sara's game

Ernie Lindsey

©2012 by Ernie Lindsey

ISBN-13: 978-1479369447
ISBN-10: 1479369446

"Say, '*It's just a game*,' one more time. Go on, do it. I dare you."

—*Anonymous*

CHAPTER 1
SARA

Sara was late again.

She plowed into her office, greeted by the overpowering scent of cologne and hair gel. Teddy Rutherford, the clichéd heir to the throne and obnoxious VP of Research & Development, sat at her desk using *her* PC to play that little game involving dogs, cats, and giant cannons. Her kids loved it, but she never saw the appeal.

As the VP of Marketing for a growing video game company in Portland, Oregon, it was her job to get their *Juggernaut* series into as many hands as possible. And since she'd been promoted to a marketing position after a decade of hundred-hour workweeks as a tester, then up to VP, LightPulse Productions had grossed more in the past eight months than over the previous five years.

Marketing came naturally to her, and nobody in the industry had seen her coming. She had been interviewed in numerous magazines, made it into the upper half of multiple Top 40 Under 40 lists, and signed a contract to write a monthly column for *Professional Mother*. All while raising twin girls and their younger brother, alone, since the day their father left for the gym and never came back.

She'd been wined and dined with some incredible offers from Fortune 500 companies, but LightPulse was her home, the house she'd helped build, and she had no intention of leaving.

Even if it meant dealing with a privileged, spoiled cretin like Teddy on a daily basis.

He said, "These guys are pure genius, aren't they? Nothing but flat animation, some bright colors, and the chance to destroy the enemy with a single click. And people play it for hours. Incredible."

He was obtrusive, annoying, and infantile: a thirty-year-old man-child who had never had his dad around growing up. Jim spent more hours at the office running LightPulse than he did at home, and his three ex-wives certainly hadn't been the right women to guide Teddy toward anything resembling a respectable human being.

But the fact that he'd been brazen enough to hack into her work account was more than an invasion. She probably would've been less offended if he'd put his hand up her shirt. She took one deep breath, then another, and tucked what she *wanted* to say back into her throat. Instead, she asked, "How'd you get into my system?"

He ignored the question. "I mean, really, look at it. I flick, it goes *boom*, pieces of wood go flying. Flick, *boom*, done. After Juggs 3 comes out,"—*that childish nickname again*, Sara thought—"we should look at going in this direction. Cut some of the staff, cut some costs. Get in good with Apple. Dad said—I mean *Jim* said—they were dying to work with us. Put something like this up on the App Store, charge a buck apiece? We can all retire and sip some boat drinks and swap wives." He winked at her.

She looked down at the heavy crystal paperweight on her desk, wondering how big the dent in the side of his head would be.

"You're trying too hard, Teddy. Now get away from

my computer and out of my chair."

Teddy stood up, lifted his hands in apologetic resignation, and then squeezed her shoulder as he walked around to the other side.

God, this guy is a harassment lawsuit wearing a fake Rolex. If he ever tried that with some of the hardcore gamer girls out in The Belly, he'd be toast.

"Sorry," he said. "You shouldn't leave your password written on a sticky note. And you're late. I got bored."

"Still not okay, Little One." Being the youngest member of the executive team—and the owner's son—was more of a scarlet letter than a badge of honor, and they all knew that the nickname was the perfect way to knock a couple inches off Teddy's platform loafers whenever he got out of line. Vertically challenged (as he insisted he was, often), he had to look up a good three inches at Sara on the days he came into the office wearing unprofessional flip-flops.

He straightened the collar of his polo shirt, smoothed out his khakis, and gave a snort of disapproval, but nothing more.

Sara smirked.

Putty.

She laid her tattered and thinning leather briefcase on her desk and took her time unpacking, making Teddy wait on purpose, letting his impatience and ADHD reach a festering point. She was poking the badger, of course, but it was justifiable retribution, and he stayed silent.

And while 'guilt' wasn't a word in his vocabulary or a feeling that had ever impregnated the three brain cells he had floating around in that all-too-polished, bronzer-coated melon, she figured he was at least aware that he'd done something wrong by invading her privacy.

She sat, pulled a notepad out of her desk, and chose a pen from her cup with such slow deliberation that Teddy was almost vibrating by the time she finally said, "I can't come up with a marketing plan without a product. So tell me, why are you two months behind?"

The direct, personalized blame was enough to send Teddy into a barrage of excuses that lasted for over an hour.

***

By the time he was done—and by the time she had tortured him to the point where it was no longer fun—they'd worked out a plan that they could take to Jim. A few extra hours per employee on Teddy's side would get them both back on schedule in another month, and Sara would have what she needed to begin a viral marketing campaign. If everything worked out as it should, *Juggernaut 3* would demolish the success of its previous two releases, but they had to be ready. Public outcry over production delays was never a good thing, and Sara had no experience in handling the backlash. Nor did she want any.

Teddy got up, but before he could leave, Sara stopped him at the door. "Teddy," she called after him.

"What?"

"If I ever catch you on my PC again..."

It was all she needed to say. He hung his head, examined the tops of his shiny Kenneth Coles, and muttered a doleful, "Won't happen again," before he escaped the prison yard of her office.

After he walked out, her assistant, Shelley, poked her timid, dimple-cheeked face around the corner. Sara smiled and motioned for her to come in. Shelley crossed through the doorway, one halting step at a time, like she was testing the ground for landmines.

Sara had never raised her voice at the poor girl, but she always approached Sara as if she would explode and send her running from the office coated in curse words and insults. Shelley was shy to the point of having trouble interacting with the outside world, but she was a brilliant marketer, and had a way with copywriting that could convince a politician to refuse campaign funding.

She worked more hours than anyone in the building, constantly refining ad copy and press releases, searching for the perfect words to tell LightPulse's story, studying the advertising giants of the past like David Ogilvy and John Caples. More than once Sara had found her asleep at her desk after pulling an all-nighter. For the past two months, the girl had been a perpetual motion machine when it came to her job, but her social life consisted of leaving her apartment on Sunday morning to brave the lines at Voodoo Doughnut and Powell's.

Sara was positive that Shelley was the smartest person in the office, and had tried to convince her of that once, but the recent San Diego State University grad had refused to accept the compliment. It had been the first and only time she had shown signs of confidence regarding something she believed in—however misguided her intent might have been, in Sara's view.

Still, her genius, under Sara's guidance, was a major

factor in the success of their advertising and marketing campaigns for their last release. If and when Sara decided to move on, she planned to ask Jim to promote Shelley over some of the other, more-seasoned team members as her replacement. But that would all depend on Shelley's ability to leave her fears behind. Sara was working on her. Slowly.

Any nudge to Shelley's delicate nature that was too forced, too forward, would tilt her in the wrong direction. Sara had seen it before, and was careful in her attempts to build up her introverted assistant's confidence.

Sara said, "How's it going, Sarge?" The shortening of Shelley's last name, Sergeant, seemed to please her the first time Sara had used it, so it stuck, and she'd been 'Sarge' ever since.

Shelley's voice came out a notch above a whisper. "Jacob's school called. They said it was urgent."

Sara tensed. The last time they'd called, he'd fallen off the monkey bars and had come home with a knot the size of a golf ball on his forehead. She said, "And you didn't forward the call? Did they say what it was about?" and knew at once that it was a little too brusque.

Shelley backed away a step, fiddling with the ruffles on her blue top. "I'm so sorry, Mrs. Winthrop. You were busy with Teddy and I knew the meeting was important and I didn't want to interrupt and—and—"

"Hey, no, it's fine. You didn't do anything wrong. Could just be another beetle stuck up his nose." *That* particular visit to the doctor caused a lot of chuckles around LightPulse, and the other employees began referring to him as 'the little bugger'. *"How's the little bugger doing?*

Pick any buggers out of his nose lately?" At the age of five, boys do what boys do.

Shelley said, "The principal called this time, not the school nurse." Admitting that it was more important than a bug up the nose made Shelley take another step back, just in case.

"What? Really? Did she say what it was about?"

"No, but she was super frustrated when I wouldn't let her talk to you right away." Shelley backed up all the way to the door.

"Weird," Sara said. "I'll give her a call. Thanks for being a good gatekeeper. But," she added, "it's okay to put a principal through during a meeting. Broken bones, too. Bugs, not so much."

Shelley acknowledged the ruling with a meek grin. Once she'd retreated, Sara dialed the school, wondering what kind of trouble Jacob had gotten into that warranted a call from the principal.

***

"Hello, Mrs. Bennett's office, Dave speaking."

"Dave, hi, it's Sara Winthrop, Jacob's mom? My assistant said—"

"Oh thank God, I'll put you right through."

Whoa, what? What's going on?

The up-tempo blast of the on-hold music didn't help her building tension while she waited. Thirty seconds passed, a minute, two minutes. She tried to distract herself by going through her email.

Mrs. Bennett's voice came on the line. She sounded

rushed, out of breath. "Mrs. Winthrop? Hello? Are you there?"

"Yes, here," Sara said, turning away from Jim's request for an all-hands meeting at 10AM out in The Belly. It was her favorite place in the building, the open-cube hub of LightPulse where she had spent so many years with the programmers and testers looking for glitches and offering suggestions on the fluidity of gameplay. "What happened? Everything okay with Jacob? Your receptionist sounded worried."

"We have a bit of a situation." The word 'situation' was loaded with unease.

"A situation?"

"Please stay calm, because we think everything is fine."

Sara sat up straight and leaned into the coming news. "You *think*? He's not hurt, is he?"

Mrs. Bennett said, "I'm sure it's nothing to worry about. It's crazy around here on the last day of school. The kindergarten classes were all outside playing hide and seek and when Mr. Blake rounded up his kids for a head count, Jacob wasn't with the rest of the group."

Sara sprang out of her chair, then tried to compose herself with a couple of deep breaths before she said, "Have you found him yet?"

The pause on the other end of the line was longer than Sara expected. "No," Mrs. Bennett said, "but we have every available adult looking. Our assistants, our teachers—even the janitor, Mr. Burns. We're positive he didn't realize that he wasn't supposed to be hiding anymore. We'll find him, but I think it's best that you come down anyway."

"I'm walking out the door right now."

Sara hung up the phone, grabbing her keys and her purse. A delicate blanket of fear enveloped her, but she tried not to let it take control. He had done this once before, months ago, when the four of them were playing hide and seek in the house. He'd climbed under a dusty green tarp down in their basement and had managed to fall asleep while she and the girls hunted for over an hour. She'd panicked and had come close to calling the police before Callie accidentally stepped on him.

Without that particular instance as a buffer, she would've been throwing people out of her way. Instead, she took a long swallow from her water bottle and then walked over to Shelley's desk to let her know what had happened and where she was going.

She heard Shelley mumbling into her headset, saying, "Yes...Oh wow, you're the second one today...Let me send you to her—oh, wait, here she is."

Sara raised her eyebrows. "For me? Who is it?"

Shelley covered the mouthpiece, saying, "Mr. Brown? Says he's the principal at Lacey and Callie's school?"

"Him, too?" *What's up with my kids today? Sheesh.* "Okay if I take it here?"

Shelley nodded.

Sara picked up the receiver, pushed the button for Line 1, and said, "Mr. Brown? This is Sara Winthrop, Lacey and Callie's mother."

The conversation that followed left the phone dangling from its cord, and at least one blindsided coworker lying flat on his back. There may have been more. It was all so blurry.

Sara flung open the glass entryway doors and sprinted down the sidewalk toward the parking lot. The sun had broken through, evaporating the morning's rain, creating a level of humidity that made the air syrupy and hard to breathe. Added to that was the realization that without her husband, she had no one to help.

I need you, Brian. Damn it, I need you. Why aren't you here when I need you?

Two years after Brian's disappearance, she'd been able to release her grip on the anxiety and fear and panic that had plagued her for days, for weeks, for months. Over time, sleepless nights dwindled to sleepless hours, and then lessened to troubled dreams and reluctant acceptance. But now, as the soles of her flats slapped against the concrete, the idea that her children might be taken from her fueled those long-subdued emotions like a gust of wind through a forest fire.

Not again, not again, not again. I can't go through this again.

A flash of white under her minivan's windshield wiper caught her attention. She thought it was another flyer for the local pizza place and ripped it from the rubbery grasp, ready to crush it in her fist.

The neon-orange, bold lettering was just bright enough to stop her squeezing hand, saving the paper slip from turning into a crumbled mass.

Seven words, asking a question that created even more questions:

ARE YOU READY TO PLAY THE GAME?

CHAPTER 2
SARA

Sara opened the driver's side door and climbed in, numb from the tips of her toes to the top of her head. Lacey, Callie, and Jacob, all three missing and unaccounted for at their schools. And now this message, whatever it was.

Her heart strained against the wall of her chest, the rhythmic thumps pounding in her ears. She needed to be on the move. Going, going, going. But the note felt like it held a deeper, more threatening meaning than a few words asking a simple question.

She stared down at the slip of paper, reading it over and over.

Are you ready to play the game? Are you ready to play the game?

Are you ready? Are you ready? Are you...

She looked at the back side, expecting to find something else, a message saying, *Just kidding! Good luck with the release!* But no. Nothing. Only the glaring, blazing question. It had to be coincidence, didn't it? Some ill-timed, cryptic joke being played on her by one of the LightPulse staff? Surely this ominous note didn't have anything to do with the kids disappearing, did it?

Of course it does. Don't be an idiot.

But what did it mean? The game? What game?

Sara flung the note into the passenger seat. *Jesus, not right now. I have to go, I have to go, I have to go.*

She cranked the keys and the Sienna's hybrid engine whispered to life. Before she backed out, she took one last glance at the LightPulse office. Shelley stood outside at the front doors, watching from a distance. She waved, then gave Sara a thumbs-up as if to say, *Everything is going to be okay.*

Sara paused at the subtle motion. Brian used to do the same thing every morning from the front porch as she left for work. He'd blow a kiss, give her a wave, and then a thumbs-up.

A wave, and then a thumbs-up.

But it meant nothing. Shelley's was a harmless platitude, wishing her well.

Sara forced herself to wave back, then swung the minivan out of the parking spot, and out into the lighter mid-morning commute.

***

"Come on, come on, *come on!*" she said, willing the stalled traffic in front of her to get the hell out of the way. The promise of a faster trip had been broken by road construction three blocks down, and she sat at a dead stop, wedged so tightly in between two cars that a pedestrian would have had trouble squeezing between the bumpers. "Move!"

She pounded the steering wheel with her palm. Flashed a look at the note beside her, where it lay limp and lifeless, but foreboding and full of questions. She shook her head. *Motherf—*

"Move!" she shouted again.

But her demands went unmet. And she sat, trapped in a line of cars, imprisoned inside her minivan with no way out and no course of action other than to wait until the universe changed its mind. She briefly thought of abandoning the van where it sat to take off running. She was in good shape. She could do it. Three miles every evening on the treadmill while the kids did their homework wasn't a guarantee of finishing a marathon, but it was enough to keep up her conditioning and ensure that her slowing metabolism wouldn't allow too many fresh pounds around her hips.

The thought of doing it, of jumping out and sprinting away, gave her a second to realize that she didn't know where she was going first. She had stomped on the gas pedal and *went*, eager to be moving, anxious to be heading toward whatever horrendous event was waiting, like a Marine running toward the sound of concealed gunfire.

How does one decide where to go first when two equally horrible things are happening at once?

She tried to weigh the options. Lacey and Callie's school was closer, but Jacob was the youngest. But was he really missing, or just hiding until someone found him?

No, obviously not the latter, not with the girls missing, too. And the note. The stupid, menacing note mocking her from two feet away.

Are you ready to play the game? Are you ready to play the game?

Mr. Brown, the principal of Whitetree Elementary where Lacey and Callie were finishing up their fifth-grade year, had said that a group of teachers had taken their classes to the small ice cream shop next to the school. It was a last day treat, and Sara recalled Shelley's reminder to sign the permission slip.

And, like the chaos of Jacob's game of hide and seek, the teachers had had trouble keeping up with everyone, both inside and outside the tight confines of the three-tabled, four-stooled room. Lacey and Callie were missing from the final headcount before they headed back to the school.

"Move!" Sara yelled once more as the car in front of her crept ahead. She stayed put, hoping that with a few more blessed inches, she might be able to squeeze the minivan out and go hurtling down a side street, taking the long way through the surrounding neighborhood. Distance-wise, it would be out of the way, but it was better than being stalled where she was.

From what she gathered, all three had gone missing around 9:00, while she was in her meeting with Teddy. Two separate instances, two separate locations, at the exact same time.

It was coordinated, she realized. *It had to have been.*

Which meant something bigger was going on than she'd originally thought. They had been targeted. She had been targeted. And it wasn't just a coincidence.

They've been kidnapped. Oh my God, oh my God, oh my God.

It was obvious, now that she had an involuntary moment to stop and think it through. Earlier she had been in such a rushed panic that she hadn't taken the time to consider the details.

Why her? Why her kids?

And who? Who would be doing this to her? To them? She tried to think of anyone who might have had any reason, and came up with nothing. There hadn't been any strange vehicles in the neighborhood lately, no ragged homeless people around their favorite park, no news reports of kidnappings that she remembered. But really, as a single parent taking care of three rambunctious children, who has time to keep track of things like whether or not the green Volvo down the street is casing the block or is nothing more than a visiting relative?

The thought brought on a rush of guilt that left her feeling like she had been punched in the stomach.

It's my fault. I should've made the time. I should've looked closer. Should've paid more attention. But how? When?

With Brian gone, it was all up to her. *She* was the one dealing with everything. The late-night accidents in bed. The homework. Proper nutrition. Cleaning the house, doing the laundry. Rushing to t-ball games and ballet classes. Everything, all of it, on her own, on top of a fifty-hour workweek. She fumed at Brian for being gone and leaving her to deal with everything.

It didn't matter where he was, where he had gone, what had happened. He was gone, and now the kids were, too. She was alone and, without a doubt, powerless.

She tried not to cry. It didn't work.

The car in front of her crept forward and Sara angled the minivan to the left, but it wasn't enough.

Come on, come one, come on. Just a little bit more.

Sara felt like she was suffocating. Rolled down the window for some fresh air, closed her eyes and inhaled. The smell came tainted with the stench of city and fresh asphalt from the paving crew up ahead. She coughed, but left the window open anyway. However stained the air might be, the sense of open freedom was better than being confined in her inability to get moving.

She waited. And waited. Her panic grew to a pulsating tremor, and she wondered if she was being punished for torturing Teddy the same way earlier that morning. Karma. Bad, bad karma.

She tried to think of anything strange that had happened over the past few days, searching her memories for some looked-over clue, some inkling of an idea as to why she and the kids would be the target of a coordinated kidnapping. At least it was some sort of action, some way of being productive while she sat immobile, taking short, fearful breaths.

Sara didn't have any enemies. Sure, she'd stepped on some toes while getting LightPulse into the national spotlight, but it was business, nothing more, and there had been no hard feelings. She was well liked—more than well liked—around all of the motherhood groups and the PTA. There was one minor instance where she'd exchanged cross words with the mother of a girl who had kept picking on Lacey, but enemies?

Enemies? It was such a strong word. And it didn't fit. Anywhere.

She thought about the park again, their walks down to Miss Willow's—the gray-haired, flowerchild babysitter. Their once-a-month trip to McDonald's for sundaes and an hour in the multi-colored indoor playground. The girls loved the slides and interconnected series of tubes where they could pretend to be hamsters scurrying from one spot to the next. Jacob spent most of his time in the ball pit, burying himself under the reds, blues, and greens, and then hurtling up and out, like a dolphin at SeaWorld, screaming with joy and his hands high in the air.

Those memories caused another series of tears, and she shifted her thoughts to the times when she was by herself.

The only time she *did* have to herself lately had been extended trips to the grocery store without the children. They were well-behaved in general, but taking them into the nearby Safeway resulted in so many admonishments to 'Put that back' and 'Stop picking out junk food for snacks' that she had given up and had began shopping after work before picking them up from Miss Willow.

Sara scanned the images in her mind, and the only thing that stuck out, the only thing that felt *off*, had been during her last trip over a week ago. She'd caught a tall, good-looking guy in a white (or was it gray?) collared shirt staring at her. She remembered amazing blue eyes. Short, dark hair. Tan skin. It'd been hard to believe that he was actually *checking her out* in her rumpled slacks and untucked blouse, looking tired and unkempt after a long day at LightPulse. They had made eye contact. It lingered. He smiled. And then he moved on.

It was the first and only time since Brian's disappearance that she had allowed herself to think, 'What if?' But she'd dismissed the thought and had gone back to picking out a fresh box of organic cereal.

Again, nothing. Nothing out of the ordinary. Nothing in her mind to make her think that it would lead to this theft, this agonizing robbery of the most important things in her life.

She grabbed her purse, pulled out her cell phone to call Miss Willow, but before she had a chance to dial, the car ahead of her rolled forward once more, leaving enough room to escape.

No more than five minutes had passed, but Sara felt like an animal released from captivity. She dropped her phone back into her purse and floored it across the southbound lane, screeching through a gap in the oncoming traffic.

A red Honda missed her rear bumper by inches. The driver blared his horn as she wheeled her way onto the side street, missing a parked motorcycle by less than a foot. She overcorrected and almost sideswiped a pickup on the opposite side. Sara fought the steering wheel, whipping her arms back and forth, and straightened out the minivan's trajectory just as an approaching car squealed to a stop. The driver glared at her. Sara crept past, mouthing, "Sorry," but his dirty look suggested that the apology wasn't accepted.

On course now, and under as much control as her frazzled mental state would allow, Sara drove as fast as she dared, working her way through the middle-class neighborhood, praying she wouldn't get pulled over. Talking to an officer at this point would be a good thing, but she didn't want to risk the delay. Not until she was ready. Not until she was at Jacob's school and was absolutely *sure* that he was gone and not taking a nap in some hidden place.

She knew that the first three hours after a child went missing were the most critical ones. The fact had stuck in her mind after reviewing the literature handed out each year by the schools. By now, as she raced through the quiet streets, she guessed that forty-five minutes had passed since her children had gone missing. Possibly longer, if it had taken awhile for the teachers to notice. They could've been gone for an hour or more already.

Sara pressed down harder on the gas pedal.

CHAPTER 3
SARA

She didn't bother with trying to find a parking spot. The minivan lurched to a stop at the front entrance to Rosepetal Elementary. She grabbed the note, shoved it in her purse, and got out, running as soon as her feet touched the ground. She flung open the wooden door, vaulted inside, and smelled the pine-scented cleaning solution. The exact same smell that had filled the halls and rooms of her grade schools back east over thirty years ago. Some things never changed.

The halls were empty. It was a huge difference from the other times she'd been here. Even when classes were in full-swing, children and parents milled about for whatever reason. Young boys with too much energy or excitement who had been excommunicated to their own island prison outside their classrooms. A mother leading her daughter by the hand, past the artwork proudly displayed along the walls. Or a group of kindergartners trudging single-file, just like Jacob had been earlier that morning, on his way out to play hide and seek.

Play. Play...

Are you ready to play the game?

But now, inside the school walls, none of those things were present. Rosepetal appeared to have been shut down. The doors of each classroom were closed, and she wondered how long it had taken them to get to that point, how long it had taken them to decide that something was wrong.

First, she checked the principal's office, in case Mrs. Bennett was there waiting for her. It was quiet and empty, as well, except for a late-twenties guy with a goatee, hipster glasses, and a flannel shirt. The typical Portland uniform.

He glanced up at her, shot out of his seat. "Mrs. Winthrop?" he asked.

She rushed up to the counter, knocked over the stack of mail. He tried to greet her as a volley of questions flew out of her mouth. Uncontained. Unrestrained. "Are you Dave? Have you found him yet? Where is everyone? Are they all out looking? Do you guys have *any idea* where he is?"

He scratched his cheek, then ran a hand across his shaved head.

She asked, "You don't, do you?" and the realization fell from overhead like a dropped piano. "You idiots. How could you let this happen?"

Dave appeared to know that this would be coming. In a calm, apologetic tone, one that sounded like it took no offense at the accusation or insult, he said, "I'm sorry, Mrs. Winthrop. I can't even begin to imagine how hard this must be, and I won't patronize you by telling you to calm down. That would be stupid—"

"Damn right it would be stupid," she said with enough contempt to keep him planted behind his desk, where it was safe.

He nodded. He'd probably seen enough irate mothers to recognize when it was time to tuck his tail between his legs and be the beta male of the situation.

"We're wasting time. Where's Mrs. Bennett?"

"She and the rest of the available staff are in back of the school, still looking. The classroom teachers are following our standard policy. We're officially locked down. You know, in case this was something—in case there was somebody—oh, man, that's not coming out right. In case something had happened to—"

"Dave?"

"Yes?"

"Shut up."

"Yes, ma'am."

"I want you to call the police."

"Mrs. Bennett said that wouldn't be necessary yet, not until—"

"If you don't pick up that phone and dial 9-1-1 in about three seconds, I'm coming over this counter and I'm going to rip that goddamn earring out of your head. You understand me?" It seemed like such a random thing to threaten him with, but it was the first noticeable item that stuck out as a source of pain. She surprised herself with the intensity, and apologized. Then she said, "You know that *something* you were babbling about? It's happening. My daughters are missing from their school, too, so I want you to call the police, have them send someone to Whitetree, and get someone here. Tell them I think they've been kidnapped, and it's been an hour."

She didn't wait for a response.

Sara sprinted out of the office, down the hallway, and through the doors that led to the rear playground.

***

Out back, some of the staff looked up into trees while some looked under parked cars on the nearby street. Others worked in pairs, walking up and down the sidewalk, calling out Jacob's name, checking the yards of homes across the way.

Sara shouted, "Jacob? Mommy's here," in a feeble attempt. "Time to come out now."

Mrs. Bennett—Wanda to those familiar enough to call her that—stood by the merry-go-round, surveying the action from her post. She was a large, imposing woman who had a stern demeanor when it came to disciplining the children and keeping the school running smoothly, but one-on-one, adult-to-adult, she was as an absolute sweetheart. Ready with a laugh, ready with a hug. She'd been Lacey and Callie's principal, too, and had even brought a tray of lasagna by a week after Brian had gone missing. Sara liked and admired her, but had to contain the urge to scream at the woman.

She knew she needed Mrs. Bennett to be focused and ready with details. Yelling at her would solve nothing. Yelling at her wouldn't improve anything.

Sara marched over to her and could see that the woman was already sweating through her light blue blouse. The rings of perspiration made a semi-circle underneath her armpits as she held up a hand to shield her eyes from the sun.

"Mrs. Bennett!" Sara said.

Please have some news. Anything good.

Mrs. Bennett waved and rushed over, meeting her halfway. "Oh, Sara," she said, holding out a hand to shake, but changed her mind at the last second and embraced her with a hug.

Sara squeezed, and could feel the warmth of the principal's body, the dewy perspiration on the woman's back. She pulled away and asked, "Any luck?" but deep down, she knew it was pointless. Not with the girls gone, too. Not with that cryptic note. *Are you ready to play the game?*

Mrs. Bennett said, "Not—not yet. We're looking as hard as we can. He *has* to be here somewhere. No child has ever gone missing on my watch, and it's not about to happen now."

"You should call them off."

Mrs. Bennett squinted at her, trying to decipher what she'd heard. "Call them off? Why?"

"Because he's been—" She had to shove the next word out of her mouth. "—kidnapped."

Mrs. Bennett scoffed, disbelieving. "What? No, don't think that way. We'll find him, I'm sure of it. My gut says we're getting close."

But Sara could tell by the sound of her voice that Mrs. Bennett was only trying to stay positive, and, on some level, she didn't believe what she was saying, either. The fact that she was being mollified bubbled up the rage boiling in her gut, but she stopped short of grabbing the principal by the shoulders and shaking her so hard her skull would flop around like a bobble-head doll.

"It's worse than you think," she said. She told Mrs. Bennett about Lacey and Callie and how they were missing, too, how they had disappeared around the same time as Jacob. She told her about the cryptic note, and what she thought it meant.

A warm breeze blew strands of hair into Sara's face. She brushed them away, tucking them behind her ear, waiting on Mrs. Bennett to process the information.

Mrs. Bennett's mouth tried to produce a response, but no words came out. Lips and jaw and tongue working overtime, producing nothing. She'd gotten stuck in an infinite loop, the same kind of bug in a programmer's code that left a game character repeating the same action over and over.

Sara fidgeted. Every second wasted was another second gone from the fading three-hour time period that had, by now, worked its way down to less than two. But the truth was that she had no idea what to do next, where to go, whom to call. Talking to the police would be a step forward, but what then? Would they take her down to the station to answer questions, offer her a cup of coffee and an empty room? What good would that do?

She could call the phone tree set up by all the parents in their neighborhood. Tell them to keep an eye out in case the kids showed up there, by some miracle. Lacey and Callie had gotten in trouble twice for switching classes. They often wore the same outfits just to be mischievous. They were clever little pranksters...something they had inherited from their father. Was it possible they'd concocted a scheme to ditch school on the last day? Could Jacob have overheard them and decided he wanted to play their game, too?

Stop grasping. They wouldn't dare *pull a stunt like that. Would they? I mean, really? Would they?*

The hamster wheel caught traction inside Mrs. Bennett's head. She said, "But who would leave that note?"

"I have no idea."

"We have to call the police, right now."

"I made Dave do it. They should be here soon."

"Good. Good," she said. She reached up, pinched the bridge of her nose. "We should've done it sooner."

"You couldn't have known."

"No, it's my responsibility. We should've called as soon as I put everybody inside on lockdown. But—but I didn't want to worry you. And I was being stupid and too pigheaded, trying to protect my own reputation. Not on my watch, right?"

Part of Sara wanted to say, *Damn right, it was on your watch*, but the other part, the half that realized that it wasn't Mrs. Bennett's fault, said, "Don't blame yourself, blame the asshole who took them."

"I should've been more proactive," she said. Mrs. Bennett looked toward the back of the school, pointed. "The police are here. You go, we'll keep looking. And tell them they can find me back here when they're ready. I'm going to take full responsibility." She gave Sara another hug.

"That's not necess—"

"I won't be able to look at myself in the mirror. It's okay, Sara, really. Go on now. He's waving you over. Use my office if you need it."

"Mrs. Winthrop—"

"Sara's fine," she said. "Two less syllables." She gave a nervous chuckle and then regretted saying it. There wasn't time for meaningless comments that required explanation. She'd been using the aside to dispense with formalities and as a conversation starter for years, and it was a hard habit to break.

Don't ask what it means, don't ask what it means...just get to the questions.

The real meaning behind it was a running joke between her and Brian that had never gone away, even in her life without him. They'd had an argument one night, about a week after they were married, over the most efficient way to load the dishwasher. It'd escalated into a notch below a screaming match. Brian had said, 'Efficiency is the soul of wit, Sara,' and she'd replied, 'It's *brevity*, ding-dong. Brevity is the soul of wit, and it's more efficient, because it's two less syllables.'

From that day on, whenever an impending disagreement was about to get out of hand, one of them would say, 'Two less syllables,' and it would diffuse the situation.

Detective Jonathan Johnson grinned at her and scribbled something on his notepad. "I know we're in a hurry here, but if it makes you more comfortable, you can call me 'DJ.' You know, for Detective Johnson. Or

JonJon, if you're a four-year-old boy, like my nephew."

"That helps," she lied.

"I don't know why I tell people—"

Sara interrupted. "Can we get started? Sorry, I'm sure it's—time is sort of..." Anxious, she rubbed her damp palms on her pants.

His cheeks took on a light shade of pink. "Of course, of course."

They sat across from each other in Mrs. Bennett's office, uncomfortably perched on the straight-backed, hard-as-a-church-pew chairs used by parents, or unruly students as they were dealt their punishments.

Detective Johnson, *DJ*, was younger than she had expected. Younger than she'd hoped for, and she wondered how recently he'd been promoted to his position. With her children gone, her world exploding around her, she wanted the best. Someone with experience. Someone with more successful cases filed away in the 'Solved' drawer than ones gone cold. She wanted her own Dream Team with Michael and Magic and Larry.

Instead, sitting opposite of her was a mid-thirties guy who looked like he might have earned his detective's badge within the last six months.

Christ, they sent a Boy Scout to look for my kids. Unbelievable.

DJ leaned forward. "What're your children's names?"

"Lacey and Callie. They're twins. Ten years old. And then Jacob. He's five."

"Okay," he said, taking notes. "To the best of your knowledge, when did your children go missing, Sara?"

"Best guess, around nine o'clock this morning, based on what the principals told me. You have someone at

Whitetree, don't you?" She squirmed in her seat, feeling guilty that she couldn't be in both places at the same time.

The young detective scribbled again on his notepad. "We do, we do. And they're in good hands over there with Detective Barker. He's been doing this longer—"

"And you've been doing it...how long?" Her heartbeat eased up at the thought of someone with experience, but she couldn't resist asking.

DJ smiled like he knew the question was coming. No doubt he'd gotten it before. "I know I look like I just started shaving yesterday," he said, "but I've been in Missing Persons for five years. All with Detective Barker. People call him Bloodhound, so you can trust me—"

"Did you have more questions, Detective?" Sara scooted forward to the edge of her seat. "I don't mean to interrupt, but my kids? Your questions?"

"Definitely. I'm in as much of a hurry as you are, so we'll get through these double-time, okay?"

"Yes, sorry, go on."

DJ cycled through the standard inquiries about how they had gone missing, had they ever run away before, any friends or immediate family who might be involved, any babysitters with less-than-stellar pasts, any enemies she might have, any strange vehicles in the neighborhood. She answered them all, being as detailed as possible, and before she could mention the cryptic note, the next question had more of an affect on her than she anticipated.

"And their father? Where is he?"

"Gone," was all she could manage.

"Gone? As in, out of the picture gone, you're divorced gone...deceased gone?" He added the last bit with some trepidation.

"I guess not talking about it isn't an option, huh?"

"If you think he could be a person of interest, we need those details so we can explore every possible alternative."

Before she could realize how ridiculous the notion might be, the possibility of Brian being involved popped into her head.

Brian? No way...Brian?

"He wouldn't," she said.

"Ma'am?"

She didn't hear the confused question. *What if it is Brian? They never found his body and people thought they saw him... Could he be involved? Could he have come back and picked the kids up? Is he on his way to the house right now, hoping to surprise me? God, that would be a cruel way to make an entrance. And after so long. I'll kick his ass back to wherever he's been, if that's the case.*

"Sara?"

"What?" Her eyes refocused, drawing her back to the present.

"Everything okay?"

"What—what was your question?"

"Your husband?"

"Right, right. Brian," she said, taking another couple of seconds to process, then added, "He couldn't be involved, Detective. He's been missing for two years."

"Missing? Do we have a file on him?"

"Two years ago, he left for the gym one morning and never came back. You guys found his car in a grocery store parking lot across from Hollywood Bowl. Said there weren't any signs of foul play, no blood, no strange DNA. No leads whatsoever. He just vanished."

"I remember that case. That was your husband?"

"Unfortunately."

"I feel like I'm doing nothing but apologizing, but I'm sorry to hear that." DJ took the opportunity to scribble on his notepad again. Cleared his throat. "I'll take a look at the files later, but right now, we really need to focus—"

A knock at the door interrupted him. "Come in," he said.

The door opened just far enough for Dave to poke his head inside. "There's a pho—"

Sara blurted out, "Did you find him?"

Dave shook his head. "Phone call for you on line two, Mrs. Winthrop."

"For me? Who is it?"

"Didn't say. Some woman. Said she needed to speak to you. You can pick it up there at Mrs. Bennett's desk."

Sara exchanged puzzled looks with the detective. "Should I answer it?"

"Yes ma'am. Could be good news."

"Oh, God, I hope you're right." She stood up, rushed over to the desk. "Hello, this is Sara Winthrop."

The voice on the other end of the line wasn't female. It was deep. Electronic. Synthesized.

It said, "The game begins now. You have twenty minutes to get to the Rose Gardens. Alone. Park. Leave your keys in the ignition and the van running. Leave all personal belongings in it. You will be given further instructions. Don't tell the police where you're going. If you need proof that this is real, pay attention."

She almost fainted when she heard the single-word scream that followed.

In her van, driving, it played over and over in her mind. *"Mommy!"*

The ensuing silence had signaled the end, and the beginning.

Sara had recognized Lacey's voice. She and Callie both sounded so much alike on the phone, but Lacey's voice was one note higher than her sister's. She was terrified, and in pain.

All of her children's voices took on a distinct tone whenever they were hurt. Call it a mother's bond, but she was able to tell the difference between the yelp of a stubbed toe and the wail of a broken arm across all three of them. Lacey's scream lay somewhere in between.

Sara's remorse bulged underneath the surface like a volcano moments before eruption.

She drove hard, taking every shortcut she could think of, dodging traffic, ducking across parking lots to avoid stoplights and long lines. She eased up on the gas pedal when she crossed paths with a police cruiser, and then floored it again when it was out of sight. She cursed the lack of acceleration in the hybrid, damning the peer pressure from her friends to go green.

Conservation had nothing to do with her circumstances, she knew, but she had to have some outlet for her rage or she risked exploding right there in her seat. With no idea as to who was behind this stupid game, she had nothing to focus her outbursts on, so taking it out on something she *was* aware of would have to suffice. For now.

At that point, she wasn't beyond choking the life out of whoever was doing this, but until that chance presented itself, cursing the environmentally conscious would suffice.

She took the Burnside Bridge and glanced down at the minivan's clock.

Ten minutes left. I'll never make it.

She wondered what Detective Johnson must be thinking or doing after her frenzied dash out of the office. She'd slammed down the receiver, the flush in her cheeks and flared nostrils revealing that the call wasn't the good news she'd been hoping for.

Before he'd been able to ask, she'd said, "I have to go. Do *not* follow me. But here's your first clue." She'd fished the note out of her purse and shoved it into his hands. "Find out where that came from. I'll call you when I can."

He'd tried to protest, but his words got lost in the rush of wind at her back.

And now, making her way across the bridge, she wished she'd had time to give him more information, to tell him what the voice had said, and to work out a plan so she wouldn't be driving into whatever was waiting for her in the Rose Gardens without backup.

Playing this so-called game on her own.

Sara thought about calling Miss Willow, just to hear a comforting voice, but there was no sense in frightening her and risk giving out too much information. But the voice had only said, *"Don't tell the police."* Should she risk letting someone else know?

No, not yet. Who knows what they'd do to the kids if they found out.

They.

Plural. Definitely more than just the person on the phone, given the timed coordination. Which meant she was up against a *group* of people. She could handle one person if she got the chance. Possibly.

Sara played it out in her mind. A well-placed kick to the balls, or a forehead to the bridge of a nose, pouncing on him with a knee across his Adam's Apple, all of her weight pressing down. It was feasible. But a group of people? No way. She imagined standing in a circle, surrounded. Imagined throwing a punch at the nearest person and then getting swarmed by a hive of vicious, grinning henchman.

She took the exit ramp and passed a young woman, bouncing lightly by on a mid-morning run.

A woman.

Why did the fact that it was a woman jogging by click in her subconscious? What was the trigger, and why did it seem important?

Dave said a woman *was on the line for me.*

Some woman.

She had forgotten that particular detail in her rush to get moving. But was it a decoy? Had they used the voice synthesizer to disguise the person's real voice as a woman's? If it *was* a woman, that narrowed the list of possibilities by half.

The kids' pamphlets said kidnappers were likely male, friends or family, and she definitely didn't know any women capable of something like this.

She had no family in the area. They were all back in Virginia. Brian had come from a small clan of Winthrops in Washington. His parents had passed. His sister lived in Des Moines. The rest of the aunts (and uncles and female cousins) stayed in the near-perpetual drizzle of Seattle. Her friends were sweethearts with children of their own. Her assistant Shelley, her coworkers, and all the rest of the women at LightPulse were good-natured and friendly. And she hadn't gotten a hint of resentment from any of them when she had been promoted to Vice President over some of the more seasoned employees. What would be their motivation?

It couldn't be anyone she knew, could it?

Behind closed doors, Sara...

No. No, no, no. It wasn't possible. Nobody close. It had to be a stranger. Had to.

But what if it wasn't?

She drove up Knob Hill toward the Rose Gardens, getting closer and closer, rifling through the possibilities, checking off each woman she knew, dismissing them all for different reasons. Most would be at work, leading busy lives. Some were stay-at-home moms keeping control of toddler-induced bedlam with no time to plan a coordinated kidnapping.

That wouldn't stop any of them from making a phone call, but none of them have a reason. Not a single one of them would have any reason to do this...would they?

Chapter 5
Sara

Sara arrived at the Rose Gardens with a minute remaining on her deadline. She found a parking spot, got out, and left the keys in the ignition with the minivan running, as instructed.

She stood with her arms crossed, taking in the surroundings. She didn't know what she was looking for, but it seemed like the right thing to do. She'd only been there once before, twelve years ago. It was on her first date with Brian, and they'd come up here after lunch and a matinee showing of *Gladiator*.

It was also the place where they had shared their first kiss. If Brian *did* have anything to do with this, it would be an appropriate spot. She shoved the thought away. Creating red herrings for herself would only increase her tension, and she had to keep a clear head for what was coming.

In front of her, rose upon rose upon rose drank in the sunlight. Such a happy, peaceful existence they had, with nothing to do but sit around all day and be admired. Thousands of cars flocked here each month to admire the amazing expanse of flowers, and today was no different. The tourist season had the entire area full and the place was flooded with visitors wearing sandals over knee-high black socks and pink plastic sun visors. Milling about with their oohs and aahs, taking happy family photographs on their happy family vacations.

It was easy to be jealous.

Why such a crowded place? They wouldn't do anything here with so many people watching, would they?

She didn't have to wait long for her answer.

A white sedan with heavily tinted windows stopped in front of her. A tall man wearing a black ski mask, jeans, and a green hoodie leapt out, took two steps toward her, and thrust a piece of paper in her hand. He towered over her, but she caught a glimpse of piercing blue eyes in their fleeting connection. Then, as the white sedan pulled away, he moved past Sara and climbed into her minivan. The entire exchanged lasted less than five seconds, and the likelihood of someone noticing a masked man was minimal.

He backed out, almost clipped Sara's knees.

"Wait!" she said, but stopped short of screaming for help. That might break the rules of the game, whatever they were.

The messenger drove away, slipped off the ski mask. Sara tried to get a better look, but had little luck. The only thing she saw was the side of his face. A normal ear. A normal head. The strands of hair were short and dark. It could've been anyone, and it definitely wasn't someone she recognized, as if that were possible from such a quick glimpse.

Sara looked down at the folded slip of paper in her hand. Before she opened it, revealing whatever instructions awaited, she tried to examine it for any hints. The hand it had come from had been gloved, so fingerprints were out of the question. Folded, it was about three inches wide and three inches long. Standard white, no lines, taken from a printer. A crisp crease along the edge. Nothing extra, nothing like an identifying watermark.

It was just a stupid piece of paper.

A link between her and the game. A link between her and rescuing her children.

It felt dense, like holding a brick.

Inside the single piece of paper were an infinite number of possibilities, an infinite number of outcomes. The thought reminded Sara of the instruction manual that came with the open-world, open-adventure setting of *Juggernaut 2*, in which players were presented with thousands of options as they grew their characters from basement-dwelling couch potatoes into heavily armed, alien-slaying behemoths. Hundreds of different quests were offered as ways to increase their strength and agility, to gather up bigger and stronger weapons, to live out fantasies of turning themselves into something they could never become in real life. It didn't matter where they went or what route they took to get there, as long as the main quest was completed: save Earth.

But Sara's game had a different objective, one that couldn't be outlined with fancy fonts and clear directions.

She opened the folded paper and read:

FIND SHAKESPEARE

Find Shakespeare? Really? That's it? What does that even mean, find Shakespeare?

She wasn't sure what she had been expecting, and she knew it wouldn't be easy, but this? These two words of confusing...nothingness?

Where in the hell were the *real* guidelines? It wasn't like the games she was familiar with. The games she had tested for LightPulse for months and years at a time. The games that had a distinct mission with accomplishable goals that you could mark off of a checklist. A save point where you were allowed unlimited do-overs, and could attack the game again with new knowledge about the possible outcomes.

LightPulse worked hard at creating an acceptable level of artificial intelligence for the enemy combatants, but technology only allowed so much. And in the end, the objectives were the same. Go here, do this, pull that lever, jump over the gap, kill that two-headed, slimy alien with saliva-coated fangs and dual laser pistols. Destroy the mothership.

Real world, Sara. Real world, different game. No easy rules. If you screw up, you can't go back to the save point and start over.

Find Shakespeare.

Two words that held no meaning to her. Did it mean that she should find a collection of his plays? Would she have to walk back to the library? She tried to remember if there were any productions going on somewhere in town, or an exhibit at a museum.

Precious seconds faded away and nothing came to mind.

They sent me here *for a reason. Shakespeare. Shakespeare. Find Shakespeare. A rose by any other name... Romeo and Juliet? Is that right? Shakespeare...roses...roses... Isn't there...*

A faint memory skittered across her mind. She spun around, searching, searching, and then ran into the garden entrance, down the pathway, and then stopped in front of the park map. An arrow pointed the way to the Shakespeare Garden.

***

From where she stood, her destination was in the back right corner of the park.

She moved. Not quite walking, not quite running. If it mattered, if it was a condition of the game, she didn't want to draw too much attention to herself. Would any of these people remember a harried woman in a rush? Doubtful. They were too wrapped up in ogling the flowers and taking pictures to see that she was one heartbeat away from frantic.

Stay calm. How does that saying about the duck go? Calm on the surface, paddling like hell underneath? If there's an endgame, you can beat it.

But why a game? That has *to mean something. Okay, it has to be someone that knows you work at LightPulse. This whole game thing isn't a coincidence.*

She passed the spot where Brian had first leaned in, where she had first closed her eyes. Under different circumstances, she would've stopped and taken a minute to say a little prayer for his return. But living in the past and tossing a coin into the wishing well of the future wouldn't get her any closer to recovering what she had left of him. And that was Lacey, Callie, and Jacob.

They were all that mattered.

She approached the Shakespeare Garden and slowed to a walk. The nervousness of stepping into a place that was too quiet was second nature to her after spending thousands of hours testing games. Step into a quiet, unsuspecting room looking for a reward, and enemies would inevitably attack.

But no such ambush awaited her. She stood near the entrance, and saw that the foot traffic within the Shakespeare Garden was light, and none of the flower-gazers appeared interested in her or her arrival.

Now what? Do I just wait? Should I squawk like a chicken and flap my arms, you shitheads?

Rather than making a fool of herself, she announced, "I'm here," into the open space.

A middle-aged couple nearby gave her a curious look, then an older gentleman responded with an energetic, "Congratulations!"

Smartass.

She stood in place, waiting. Waiting. Waiting long enough to think that she could've been wrong, and this wasn't the Shakespeare she was supposed to find. The muffled sound of a ringing phone came from somewhere behind her. She expected one of the men or women nearby to answer, but it kept beckoning.

Is that for me?

The sound was close. She pivoted around to look for it, saw the Shakespeare plaque on the brick wall. A bust of the great bard and a quote that read, *Of all flowers, methinks a rose is best.*

Below it sat an inconspicuous collection of twigs, leaves, and small rocks. She knelt down, rummaged through the pile and uncovered a silver, older model flip-phone.

She flipped it open, answering with a subdued, "I'm— I'm here."

"Welcome to the first level, Sara. I like to call it...*Humiliation.*"

CHAPTER 6
SARA

"There will be three levels. One for each child. Complete all three successfully and you *may* win."

"I *may* win?"

"That depends on whether or not your prince and princesses are in another castle." The voice giggled, and digitized, it sounded even more sinister.

Sara caught the *Super Mario* reference. It had been one of her favorite games as a child. The long hours she spent mastering it, collecting coins and squashing mushrooms, were some of the happiest memories from her youth, but also some of the most maddening. Screams of frustration, followed by flying Nintendo controllers and a broken television screen had resulted in more than one grounding and innumerable parental sanctions against playing it, but they never lasted long, because her parents couldn't resist the squeals of delight when she was winning.

She surveyed the area around her. No one was paying attention. She said, "Listen, I don't know who you are—"

"No, Sara, *you* listen."

A short silence, followed by an "*Owww!*"

Her son this time.

It made her feel dizzy.

The voice said, "Did you hear that?"

Sara ground her teeth. "Yes."

"Try to defy me again. I *dare* you."

"I won't. I—I promise. Just don't hurt him again.

Please?"

"That depends on how you play the game, Sara. There are rules, and in this case, they're *not* meant to be broken. Do you understand?"

"Yes, but what—can I ask what they are?"

"You'll figure them out as you play. Be aware, mistakes are costly, and there are no breakaways in this game."

Breakaways. What did that mean? Breakaways? That's a Juggernaut term.

Sara's mind raced. This twisted chick on the other end of the line, whoever she was, was familiar enough with their flagship game to know that a 'breakaway' was a power-up bonus that allowed a player to set off a mini-bomb and obliterate everything within a city block, thus evading capture or death from an advancing army of alien beasts.

If it's a she.

But was the mention of it a slip-up? Or was it intentional? Was it enough to be a clue?

LightPulse prided itself on their strong female following. Just because one of them was acquainted enough with the product to use a recognizable term didn't mean a damn thing. That narrowed the possibilities down to thousands and thousands of women all across the world. Especially in Japan. The current trend in the Japanese sub-culture of gamer girls was to get tattoos of their avatars on their lower backs, and to call them insane fans was an understatement.

But it was nothing concrete. The net was too wide.

Then, a revelation opened up in her mind like a house window during a hurricane.

The breakaway feature wasn't being introduced until

-43-

the *third* installment of *Juggernaut* was released. Which was still in development. Which was still under lock and key. Which was still protected by non-disclosure agreements throughout the whole company.

It's somebody from LightPulse. Holy shit, that mini-bomb idea was Teddy's!

As the blast of information shook her like she'd been hit by a mini-bomb herself, the voice interrupted her thoughts. "Now, are you ready to begin the first level?"

What Sara *wanted* to say was, 'Is that you, Teddy?' but rather than revealing what she suspected, she replied, "I obviously don't have a choice."

"You're right, you don't. Now listen closely, because the instructions for each level will only be given once. Your phone is being monitored. Do not try to make any calls. Keep it with you at all times and answer it as soon as it rings."

"Whatever you say."

"You are being watched. You are being followed. Don't try to figure out who it is, because that would be a waste of time. It could be the old man holding his wife's hand about twenty feet to your left."

Sara looked around. It was the same smartass who had said, 'Congratulations!' and she seethed at him, however unlikely it was that he was involved. Her tormentor was trying to make a point. There were unseen eyes focusing on her right now from somewhere in the vicinity. The hair on her arms stood up.

"Trust me, Sara, any attempts to deviate from the game's objectives will result in consequences that these little angels will not enjoy. I can assure you."

Sara wished there was a bench nearby. She needed to sit down. She said, "Whatever you say, I'll do it."

The voice chuckled. "If your children's lives weren't at stake, I'm sure you'd regret those words in a few minutes."

"Whatever it takes."

Whatever it takes, Teddy, you little shit. I should've beaten you over the head this morning when I had the chance.

"I like your spirit. It could save three lives today. Before I give you the instructions for this level, I will offer this: you will be given the chance to ask *one* question for each round. Call it a *bonus* round. You may ask at the beginning of the level or at the end. What is your decision?"

Sara hesitated, but the immediate question on her mind meant more now than it would later, once she was in too deep. She would have to trust that she could beat or solve whatever puzzle was presented to her without any help. "I'll ask now," she said.

"That may not be your best decision so early on in the game, but...proceed."

"Why are you doing this?"

The sustained silence from the voice allowed the other sounds around her to creep in. Birds chirped. Bees buzzed around the roses. Wind rustled the leaves above her. High heels clicked on the walkway. Somewhere behind her, a carefree tourist laughed.

"I suppose I could say, 'Because I can,' but what fun would that be? Here is my answer, Sara: you don't know what it is yet, but you've taken something from me, something very important, and this is only the beginning of my retribution."

What did I take from Teddy?

She'd talked down to him far too often, but it had never been malicious. Just enough to get her point across that she wasn't interested in him, or that she wasn't going to lie down and be a doormat just because he was the owner's son. Had she called him Little One too many times? Taken his manhood? Would that be enough of a motivator for him to kidnap her children and threaten their lives?

No. It couldn't be. Could it?

All the other seniors call him that, too. If that were the reason, he'd be targeting them, too.

Before she could stop herself, an instinctive response shot out. "What was it?"

A pause, and then another yelp of pain. This time from Callie. Sara covered her mouth to keep from screaming.

"You broke a rule, Sara. Only one question per round."

"Oh, God, I know, I know. I'm sorry. I'm so sorry. Just, please, don't do that again."

"This has gone on too long. I'm getting bored," the voice said, then followed it with a drawn out sigh. "So bored, Sara. I want to play *now*."

It was almost childish. Whiny. Infantile. Just like Teddy. Sara said, "Tell me what to do."

"Oh, goodie. This will be fun. Here is your objective for the first level, Humiliation. I'll admit that it's the easiest, but aren't all first levels? I don't want to break you before you get started. Now, you must strip where you stand. Remove every last bit of clothing. Walk to the center of the Shakespeare Garden and stand perfectly still for five minutes. No matter who approaches, you must not speak to them. In that time, you must solve this riddle, which will lead you to your next destination. The riddle is this: *The scarlet trusses contain the key where East meets West.* Take the phone with you. I'll call when your five minutes are up."

The call disconnected, and the voice was gone. Sara had never felt such rage against another human being. She felt like screaming at the sky and smashing the phone under her heel. She felt like tearing down the brick wall with her bare hands. She felt like ripping the head off each rose one by one, crushing their beauty within her fists.

She was under surveillance, however, and destroying the world around her wasn't an option.

Humiliation. For the kids, for the kids, for the kids. Okay. Okay, I can do this. I can do this.

She recited the riddle slowly. "The scarlet trusses contain the key where East Meets West."

Okay, figure it out later. They're watching. Five minutes. What's the worst that could happen? I get taken down by park security? Do they have security here? They could call the cops on me. Then what? Stop analyzing! You don't have time for this!

Sara took a look around her. Some of the browsers had moved on. Some were gawking at the flowers. Others had been replaced with a new gaggle of tourists.

Do it, do it, do it. You don't have a choice.

She reached up and unbuttoned her blouse. Her fingers that were once quick and nimble from a decade of clicking away on a game controller were now fumbling and clumsy. The buttons resisted escaping their slots and she grew so impatient that she ripped her shirt open and sent the last two flying into the grass. She slipped off her flats, and then took another look. No one was watching, but they would be soon enough. She took off her pants, then her bra and panties.

The warmth of the sun did nothing to save her from full-body gooseflesh as a cool breeze rushed past. She tried to cover herself, but it was about as effective as using a necktie for a blanket. One arm crossed her breasts, the other went down to the spot between her thighs.

She wasn't sure how much time had passed since the call had ended, but she was certain that it hadn't counted toward her five minutes.

Move, Sara. Go. Go now. Do it!

She stepped out onto the walkway, naked, and in no way free.

***

Sara tiptoed over to the center of the Shakespeare Garden and stopped in the middle of the path. The men close by began to sense that something was amiss, heads swiveling in her direction. Furtive glances crawled over her skin, violating and scrutinizing her body, getting a good look at the birthmark on her left thigh, the dimple on her right butt cheek, the ever so slight pudginess of her middle that would never go away, no matter how much she ran. She felt like she was being judged. Critiqued over every tiny flaw like livestock at an auction.

At least until their wives or girlfriends noticed her, too, and began urging them to look away or move on. One man tripped and fell over his dog. A woman scolded her from a distance, yelling at her to put some clothes on.

If you only knew, lady.

The only eyes that had seen her naked body in the past two years had been her own. And before that, before the twins came along, she and Brian had taken one adventurous trip down to the Cougar Reservoir where they had skinny-dipped in the hot springs that were buried amongst the waterfalls and evergreens. That was different. That was intentional. And it didn't matter so much, because everyone else lounged around naked, too, burning incense and warming themselves in the man-made pools.

But this—this was pure, unadulterated *humiliation.*

They must think I escaped from an asylum. What did I ever do to you, Teddy, to deserve this?

Sara felt the hot bricks burning the soles of her feet and shifted to remove a piece of gravel digging into her skin. How much time had passed? How much longer did she have to wait? Thirty seconds? A minute? She wondered how long it would take someone to locate an employee and tell him about the nude crackhead over by Shakespeare.

A couple of minutes tops, then another couple of minutes to call the police. I can get through this. Quit glaring at me, asshole. Take a damn picture. Lady, I know I need to put some clothes on! Stop yelling. You're going to attract more attention! Seriously, I will punch you in your fat hamburger face if you get close enough.

A younger guy wearing a bandana, showing off tattooed arms that stuck out of his basketball jersey, turned to see what the commotion was about. "Woohoo!" he shouted, and then his girlfriend slapped his shoulder.

If humiliation is the easiest level, I don't want to know what the rest of this game is going to be like. Game. Game. Damn it, the riddle! What was it again? Scarlet trusses. The key. East meets

West. Trusses. Okay, some kind of bridge. Right? A bridge? Is there a scarlet bridge around here? It has to be somewhere close, somewhere here in Portland.

Sara ran down the list of bridges that crossed the Willamette River. The Fremont. The Hawthorne. The Steel Bridge and the Morrison. Broadway and Burnside.

Scarlet. Scarlet is red. Are any of those bridges red? The Broadway Bridge is kind of red...could that be it? Yeah, but it wouldn't be that easy. He specifically said scarlet. What does scarlet have to do with any of the bridges?

Sara thought. And thought. And shifted her weight from one foot to the other as people glared and stared at her body. It was difficult to concentrate with all the turmoil going on around her. People would enter the Shakespeare Garden and pause long enough to take in the spectacle and either stand with their arms crossed and watch or rush away, covering their children's eyes.

At least you have your kids with you. You'd do the same thing. Ugh, how much time do I have left? Two minutes? Three?

A man walked up to her and stopped no more than four feet away. He smiled, and then clapped five beats. He put his hands on his hips and looked down. Sara could feel him examining her feet, looking at her chipped toenail polish. Regardless of the fact that she was completely naked, she was embarrassed by the neon pink color she had chosen over a month ago. Such a small decision to do something *fun* had resulted in a sense of self-consciousness that momentarily outweighed her nudity, even in such a public place.

I know, I know. I haven't had time to get them fixed. Now get away from me. I need to concentrate. Please. Please leave.

His gaze worked his way up her legs, over her covered crotch, across her tummy and breasts, then he looked her in the eyes. Sara didn't know whether or not he could sense her pain and unease, but his words brought on an odd sense of muted comfort. In a deep, southern drawl, he said, "I don't know what you're doing, lady, if you're plumb crazy or brave as hell, but we need more people like you in this world. This takes some balls. Bigger than mine, that's for sure."

He walked away.

Sara watched him go, wanted to beg him not to leave.

Crazy and *brave. And I'd give you a million bucks just to be wearing your baseball cap right now. What's that on the back of your hat? Is that an 'A'? Who is that? Atlanta? A big red 'A,' just like the scarlet letter. How appropriate would that be? Shame. Humiliation. I hated The Scarlet Letter. What Hawthorne put that poor woman through—oh my God.*

The Scarlet Letter. Nathaniel Hawthorne. The Hawthorne Bridge.

Wait, the bridge is green, but the railing is red. And the Hawthorne Bridge was named after some doctor...doesn't matter. That has to be it. It's too much of a coincidence. The humiliation factor. Scarlet. That's what he had in mind. The scarlet trusses contain the key where East meets West. The key he was talking about has to be in the middle, where the bridge is raised. Where East meets West.

She was so relieved she would've clapped too if it wouldn't have revealed her more intimate parts.

Now I just have to make it through the rest of the five minutes—

"Ma'am? Ma'am?!"

Sara saw a woman, a park employee carrying a walkie-talkie, striding toward her, stomping so hard she could've left footprints in the bricks.

Here we go. That didn't take long. Jesus, what'll happen to the kids if I'm in jail?

Lacey, Callie, and Jacob, hidden away somewhere, suffering at the hands of a madman. Begging for their mother. Wrists bound with rough rope on little arms. What would happen to them? What would he do to them if she got arrested, if she weren't able to finish the game? Surely Teddy had planned for something like this, had contingencies set up in case something went wrong. The game was his, and he wanted it played. It wouldn't be any fun if it was over before it started.

Twenty feet away, the park employee said, "I'm gonna have to ask you—"

The phone rang in Sara's hand. She flipped it open, held it up to her ear.

The voice said, "My contact tells me you're about to get in trouble. Laugh. Apologize. Tell her you lost a bet. Stay on the line."

Sara did as she was told. Forced a laugh and apologized to the approaching employee. "I'm sorry, I'm sorry. I didn't mean to cause a scene. I lost a bet."

"Leave. Now."

The woman reached for Sara's arm, but she twisted away and said, "I'm going, don't worry," and then dashed down the walkway toward her clothes. Into the phone, she said, "Okay, I'm clear."

"I heard. And I enjoyed that very much, Sara. You played well. Good game."

"Are the kids okay?"

"*Tsk, tsk, tsk*, Sara. Only one question per round. But I will let this one slide. It's a natural reaction, of course."

Sara approached the spot where she had taken off her work clothes, but instead, they had been replaced by a running outfit. *Her* running clothes and *her* running shoes.

He's been inside my house. How did he get past all the alarms?

The ultra-expensive security system had been installed after Brian's disappearance, in case whoever had taken him wasn't satisfied with just a single Winthrop in their collection. Aside from her and the children, who never remembered it anyway, the only other two people that she trusted with the code were Miss Willow and Shelley, who were allowed to drop by for extra sets of clothes for the kids or to pick up things she needed for the office.

Did you torture one of them to get the code, Teddy? Make them play your stupid game, too?

Sara couldn't imagine what it would've taken for one of her two closest confidantes to reveal that secret.

Shelley was fine this morning. Oh no, oh no, oh no. Willow!

The voice asked, "Did you solve the riddle?"

"Yes. The Hawthorne Bridge. In the center. Where East meets West."

"I knew you could do it. See? I told you this level would be easy. In front of you are your running clothes. You have forty-five minutes to reach your destination. When you find the key, the first level will be complete. Keep the phone. Await further instructions."

Sara dressed.

And then she ran.

CHAPTER 7
DJ

Detective Johnson, DJ, sat hunched over his desk, reading through Brian Winthrop's file. He tried to tune out the noise around him and focus, but the rustling papers and ringing phones and near constant foot traffic between the desks hindered his attempts at complete attention. He lifted his coffee cup and swallowed the last dregs of oil refinery leftovers.

Barker, a.k.a. *Bloodhound*, peered at him from over the top of his bifocals. "You could peel paint with that stuff, JonJon. Imagine what it's doing to your insides."

DJ looked up from the file. "Again?"

"Again what?"

"Again with the JonJon."

"It's your fault, cowboy. I don't know what life's like down yonder in Texas, but 'round these here parts, you don't offer a man the noose that's gonna hang you."

"You need to work on that accent. A real Texan would whip your ass just for trying."

"You're saying you're not a real Texan?"

DJ shook his head and grinned. Similar exchanges happened at least once a day, and he'd taken the ribbing as a sign that Barker was warming up to him five years later. Up until about six months ago, the most that could be said about their relationship was 'same car, same job.' But once DJ had solved a case that had perplexed even the great and mighty Bloodhound, a microscopic seam had opened in the older detective's armor. They weren't friends, yet, but at least DJ got to see what respect looked like when viewed through a pair of binoculars.

And in truth, 'respect' wasn't the right word. He felt like he deserved it, but the way Barker treated him suggested he'd yet to earn it. Not from Barker, not from the other detectives. One day, though, they'd be looking up to him. One day.

Their three-hour window had closed thirty minutes earlier. Barker had insisted that they return to the office and review the missing husband's file because his instinct said that Brian Winthrop was the catalyst. DJ had complied without question, partly out of deference to the senior detective, and partly because he'd witnessed the accuracy of Barker's initial reactions so many times that he knew that it was as reliable as the sun rising.

Barker's main mantra—the one that had resulted in so many solved cases—was simple: *Nature gave us the tools, but not all of us know how to use them properly.*

But now, with a short file and no new leads, DJ wished he'd pressed harder to get out into the field and start looking and asking questions. Rather than digging through one of the most confounding cases the department had seen in the past ten years, according to the notes, they needed to be focusing on the present. Detective Wallace, who'd retired a year ago, was so dumbfounded by the complete disappearance of Brian Winthrop that he had left the following in his records: *"Better chance of finding Amelia Earhart."*

Barker said, "Quit looking at the clock, DJ. I know what time it is," with the tolerance of a bemused grandfather. "If you hadn't let Mrs. Winthrop go, we might have a little more to guide us."

"I told you already, she handed me the note and ran out. What was I supposed to do, tackle her in the parking lot?"

"You could've tailed her. Less chance of a lawsuit."

They had been through this at least three times already. "Like I said, she asked me not to follow her." He didn't mention that she had *ordered* him not to follow her.

"Since when do you listen to somebody who could be a suspect?"

"Since *you* taught me to trust my instincts. And she's not a suspect."

"People lie, DJ—"

"'*Even when they think they're telling the truth.*' I know that, Barker, but whatever it was, it had to do with that note and her kids. No question."

"She could be dead by now."

DJ didn't have a response for that, but he hoped it wasn't true. He looked down at his desk, at the note Sara had found on her windshield, safely contained in a plastic evidence bag.

Are you ready to play the game?

He held it up and asked, "So what do we have here? What is this?"

Barker took off his glasses, and began chewing on the earpiece. "Conundrum," he said. "It's a sign that we're dealing with something other than a run-of-the-mill kidnapper who's looking for some kind of ransom. What we have is a sociopath who's looking to toy with this woman. He's playing a game—for lack of a better word—

and if it means what I think it means, he's smarter than your average wannabe who'll make mistakes."

"What do you think it means?"

"He created the game, he can change the rules. That, cowboy," he said, "does not bode well for us, nor for Mrs. Winthrop, I'm afraid."

"You think it's the husband? Is that why we're sitting here going through this useless report?"

"Patience, Speed Racer. What I *know* is that when it comes to cases like this—"

"*Coincidences put the bad guys behind bars and keep the paychecks coming.*" DJ huffed, and then laid the note back down on the desk. He stared at it, thinking about the interview with Sara, and the call that came for her. "One question."

"One answer."

"You keep saying *he*, but how do we know it's not a *she*? The receptionist at the school said a woman was calling for Sara."

"*Mrs. Winthrop.* Don't get too close. Could've been an accomplice. You should know that. And besides, the statistics say the ratio is something like eight-to-one, male to female. Numbers don't—"

"*Numbers don't lie, people do.*"

"And the sooner you learn that, the easier my job will get. Get back to Mr. Winthrop's file. We're missing something." He leaned back, repositioned his glasses, and resumed reading. The only way he could've looked more relaxed would be with the addition of a pipe, a smoking jacket, and a pair of expensive slippers. Throw in a roaring fireplace and a mahogany bookshelf for good measure.

Sniffing down the wrong path, Bloodhound. We're wasting time.

But he let it go. With zero solid leads and an absent mother who wouldn't answer her phone, they had nowhere to rush off to. He and Barker both complained about how unhelpful the interviews were with the staff at both schools. And the babysitter, Willow Bluesong, wasn't answering his calls, either, and hadn't been home when they'd stopped by on their way back to the station.

DJ resigned himself to giving the file one more pass and decided that when he was done, he was going to LightPulse. With or without Barker.

***

Brian Jacob Winthrop had just turned 38 at the time of his disappearance on a Friday morning in May. He was two years older than his wife Sara, and a father to twin girls and one boy. He'd worked reasonable hours as a financial analyst for a small investment company, operating his own storefront out of the east side of Portland, which was open from 8 to 5, every weekday. He ate lunch at the sub shop next door and played softball on the weekends, when the absence of familial obligations allowed for it. Athletic center records indicated that he swam for an hour each Monday, Wednesday, and Friday, and he hadn't missed a workout on those days in five months. The week he'd missed before that was the result of a conference in San Diego, according to his wife.

He had no prior record, except for two speeding tickets. Had no outstanding debts, no mortgage, and they were financially comfortable, if not well to do, in some respects. He'd struggled to gain new customers during the recession, but invested his existing clients' money wisely. No lost money, no bad blood to be found there, either.

No gambling addictions, no transaction records from strip clubs. No reason to be involved in the shadier side of society. His wife, Sara, had admitted that they'd smoked marijuana once, on their honeymoon, and hadn't touched anything since. Drugs weren't a factor, and they rarely drank, so alcoholism and its detrimental effects weren't a likely culprit. They had disagreements over finances and obligations like most couples, but none had been recent, and nothing that would've created the need to skip town.

From what DJ gathered, the guy had been a normal husband and father, completely clean.

He remembered another one of Barker's refrains. *'Nobody's a whistle, DJ,'* which he took to mean that nobody was as *clean* as a whistle. Sometimes his partner's attempts at being a wise old sage got in the way of the actual message.

Could that be it? Was he too clean? Is that what Barker's looking at? I'm not seeing a damn thing.

DJ flipped to another page.

Winthrop had packed up his workout gear that morning, kissed his wife goodbye, and then left for the gym. That was the last time Sara had seen him, and three days later, his BMW hatchback had been located in a grocery store parking lot. There were no odd fingerprints: only his, his wife's, and those of their three children. No secondary DNA traces, no blood, no out of the ordinary hair samples. No signs of forced entry on the car. No signs of foul play whatsoever.

The only strange thing that Detective Wallace had noted was the fact that the car was so clean on the inside, and it looked like it'd been washed as recently as that day. He'd reasoned that the car of a father with three young children should be filled with cracker crumbs, errant french fries, and enough dirt to cover a baseball diamond. Wallace had checked credit card transactions for any car wash visits in an effort to set up a timeline of his whereabouts, but came up empty.

No money was ever removed from their bank accounts, and no additional pings on credit card usage had ever turned up. His side of the closet contained every bit of clothing he owned. Wherever Brian had gone, the only things that went with him were his keys, his wallet, his gym bag, and the sweat suit he was wearing when he walked out the door.

Except for a number of unreliable sightings, Brian Winthrop had evaporated.

"Barker," he said.

His partner looked up from his copy of the report.

"I got nothing. The guy's a ghost, man. *Poof*...gone."

Barker said, "You're partly right."

"How so?"

"He's gone."

"Gone where?"

"Anything in those reported sightings look fishy to you?"

"Other than the fact that they're unreliable?"

"Take another look."

DJ hated it when Barker made a point of testing him, but he played along. He checked the list again. "Outskirts of Portland, the day after they found his car. Somebody thought they saw him in Eugene after that. Grants Pass. Eureka. The last one was in San Francisco, three weeks after he disappeared. Who'd remember to be looking for some guy three weeks later?"

"And?"

"And what, Barker? Six feet tall, brown hair, brown eyes. Great, we just narrowed our options down to half the male population in the US. It could've been anybody. You say it all the time—what people see and what they think they see are two completely different things."

"We're supposed to question their reliability, JonJon. That's what we're here for, but you gotta understand that the mind makes connections," Barker said, pointing at his temple. "It's a dang complex computer. What sticks out to me—and what you should be seeing, too—is that if these sightings were real, he might've been heading *south*. Why was he hightailing it south? That means something."

DJ shoved himself up from the desk, grabbing his badge and gun. "This is pathetic," he said. "When the *real* Barker shows up, the one that doesn't make assumptions based on complete nonsense, let me know. I'm going to look for this woman's children that are missing *right now*, not some guy who vanished two years ago."

"The signs are there, DJ. It's connected somehow. Why? Why would he be going south?"

"Because that's how the news traveled, Barker. People saw his picture on television, it created an image in their brain, and then they *thought* they saw him at a gas station the next day, when in reality it was some random guy on his way to work. You keep chasing your tail. I'm going to

LightPulse."

The approaching Sergeant Davis blocked DJ's dramatic exit. He said, "Barker, you and the cowboy here need to get up to the Rose Gardens. Report just came in about some crazy naked woman there that fit Sara Winthrop's description."

DJ thanked him, then said to Barker, "Well?"

"Sounds like the game's already started. Okay, you head over to her office, I'll go check out the Gardens. But this doesn't mean the mister is off the table, got it? And drop that note off at the lab on your way out, see if they can find some prints."

He nodded, and offered a curt salute.

Naked at the Rose Gardens? What kind of game are you playing, Sara?

CHAPTER 8
SARA

Sara's feet pounded the pavement. She ran as fast as she dared down the hill, away from the Rose Gardens, away from her humiliation, cutting through the trees. The shortcut was more dangerous than taking the winding, looping road all the way to the bottom, but it would save her valuable time as long as she managed to keep from rolling an ankle. A sprain would be disastrous, but it was a risk she had to take.

She reached Sherwood Boulevard and found the opposite side blocked by a chain link fence, topped with barbed wire. "Shit," she said. "Son of a bitch."

She turned left and sprinted down Sherwood, controlling her breathing on a 3-2 count. Inhale on three steps, exhale on two. Inhale on three steps, exhale on two. Cars crept past and she examined each one, looking for someone that might be watching her, keeping an eye on her progress. Not a single driver gave her more than a passing glance. She risked a look over her shoulder, examining the road behind her for the white sedan with tinted windows. Her only tail was the Gray Line trolley with wooden seats and pink trim.

If the goons in the white sedan *were* trying to track her, they probably hadn't expected her to cut straight down the hill, and thus they hadn't been able to catch up yet.

She passed a parked, City of Portland work truck and then the chain link fence to her right melded into a wrought iron one, painted black. Below it, and on the other side, was one of the many reservoirs stationed around the hill. Once she reached Washington Way, she turned right onto the sidewalk and picked up her pace.

A paved walkway carved a path through the trees to her right. She wasn't sure where it went, and rather than risk an avoidable delay, she held her course through the mossy pines.

The rhythm of her breathing began to deteriorate as her lungs burned and her quads strained to keep up. A stitch crawled its way into her left side. She backed off her pace, enough to get her breathing under control fifty yards later.

I should ease up. Can't crash so soon.

No, no whining. Think about what the kids are going through. Push harder, damn it, push harder.

She increased her speed and thought about a video that Brian had shown her about a year before he had gone missing. She'd been suffering through a bout of depression for at least two months. Work wasn't going well, Jacob was going through his Terrible Twos, she wasn't sleeping, and many, many more things that she couldn't remember. A variety of factors had lined up to take their shot at pounding on her and then everything had coalesced at once after a good reaming from Jim when her team didn't make a hard deadline.

The video itself, the one Brian had dug up on YouTube, was Jim Valvano's speech from the ESPY awards, back in the early '90s. She couldn't remember all of it, other than the fact that he was dying from cancer and the message he wanted to convey. *"Don't give up. Don't ever give up."*

Those words carved themselves into her memory like a commandment on a stone tablet, and they would resurface whenever she needed them the most, just as they were doing right then. Sara could see the images of Valvano being helped up the stairs to the podium. His smile. His tuxedo. His slicked back hair. Pleading to the crowd.

Don't give up. Don't ever give up, Sara.

She picked up her pace another notch, and figured she had to be somewhere around an eight-minute mile. Her usual speed on the treadmill was around nine and a half or ten minutes, but she had always known she could do more.

Sara took another look over her shoulder.

No white car. Maybe they weren't following. Maybe she'd lost them.

She reached a junction in the road and crossed over to read the street signs. Straight ahead, the road wound back up into the trees on Lewis Clark Way, so she turned right and ran down Park Place until she reached an intersection she recognized. She made another right on Vista and headed toward Jefferson, which would lead her directly down to the park beside the Hawthorne Bridge.

I could stop, call the police. Tell Johnson where I am.

She looked down at the phone in her hand, now slippery from her sweaty palm.

Teddy said it was being monitored. I could leave it somewhere, run into a store. Should I risk it? If I'm caught...the kids...

Sara passed parked cars and shrubbery. Staircases leading up to nice homes and hand-laid rock walls. When she reached an intersection that had Kings Court on her left and Madison to her right, she realized she'd made a costly mistake.

The Vista Bridge crossed *over* Jefferson below, where she needed to be.

She stopped and looked up the incline of the bridge, dreading the uphill trudge that would lead her across it. She tried to slow her ragged breathing, wiped the sweat from her face. Cursed herself for forgetting. Every wasted second costing her, keeping her from Lacey, Callie, and Jacob.

She sprinted to the bridge's edge and looked down the hillside.

I'll break my ankle.

The phone rang in her hand, startling her so much that she almost dropped it.

"What?" she said, and almost added, *'Teddy,'* to the end of it.

The voice said, "Why are you stopping?"

"Stopping?"

"Yes, you are stopped at the bridge on Vista, Sara, and I want to know why. You wouldn't be trying to inform someone of your...*situation*...would you?"

The creepy sensation of being *watched* hovered around her. She scanned the area and saw no white sedan, nor anyone that looked like they might be keeping tabs on her position. Looked up into the trees nearby, half expecting to see someone perched on a limb holding a camera. Instead, a squirrel twitched its tail and then scampered further up the trunk as a cyclist zipped by.

"Answer me, Sara."

"I'm just trying to figure out the quickest way. That's all."

"I sense some tension in your voice," it said. "You

wouldn't be lying to me, would you?"

"No, no, I'm not. I swear."

"Because if you are, I have some pliers in my hand that haven't pinched anything in a while."

"Don't!" she screamed, scaring another passing cyclist so much she almost ran into the curb. "If you put one more motherf—"

"Careful," the voice shot back. "Remember the rules."

"You can take your rules and—I mean, damn it. Okay, your game, your rules. I'll play."

"That's a good girl. I trust you won't get any ideas?"

"No. No ideas. I'm going, I'm going."

"Good. But as a penalty for this minor infraction, I'm reducing your time. Twenty minutes remain. The clock is ticking."

Sara slammed the phone shut.

Asshole! Okay, move. Go, go, go.

Down the hill of King street, up to Main, running, running, running hard, forcing her tired legs to get one foot in front of the other, cutting through the neighborhood, making her way back to Jefferson, and then straight ahead toward the Hawthorne Bridge.

The slight decline of Jefferson increased her momentum, but it also made for an awkward running position and caused more painful heel strikes that sent shockwaves up through her shins and into her lower back.

Pain is temporary, pain is temporary. You have no choice. For the kids, for the kids.

Sara worked her way back through her past interactions with Teddy and tried to remember what she'd done to him. All the times she had called him 'Little One'. All the times they had sat in meetings together and she'd proved him wrong. All the times she had removed his hand from some part of her body with a cautioning tone.

The number of instances where he could've taken offense were endless, but was it enough? People killed for less, didn't they?

But Teddy? He's not...he's not smart *enough for something like this.*

Sara's lungs felt like they were turning themselves inside out. Her quads and calves were melting into mush, but the adrenaline allowed her to keep pushing, pushing. Pushing past the light rail stop and across intersections. Past apartment complexes and empty office buildings.

Sweat ran into her eyes and soaked her shirt so much that it hugged her skin like a wetsuit. Feet swelling, muscles straining, but she kept putting one leg in front of the other.

No, it has to be Teddy. Has to.

Was that why he'd kept her in the meeting so long that morning? So his plan would have time to work? And he mentioned the breakaway. His baby. His idea. His big contribution. One of the rare times he'd contributed something useful to a project. One of the rare times the senior staff had given him credit instead of chiding him. He had to be throwing it back in her face. Enough of a hint to say, 'See what happens? See what happens when you push too far?'

All of it was there. The admonishments, the chiding, the years of subtle insults to pop his inflated ego.

But the more she thought about it, the longer she analyzed their past, and as she sprinted toward her destination, she couldn't shake the sensation that no matter what their history might be, Teddy Rutherford was just too lazy and self-absorbed to bother with something like this.

***

She played an impromptu, live version of *Frogger* crossing Naito, and then made a left at Riverfront Park, angling her way up the entrance ramp to the Hawthorne. Her body ached and she was so thirsty she could've buried her head into the Willamette and chugged until she regurgitated the less-than-pristine river water.

I was so sure it was Teddy, but now—

It has to be him. He's the only one with the slightest bit of motive.

But it doesn't feel right.

When would anything like this ever seem right?

I don't know, but if it is him, I'm gonna show him what 'flick, boom, done' really feels like.

She passed the line of cars waiting for their turn. The exhaust fumes polluted the air around her, leaving a thick, burnt-fuel taste on her tongue. She coughed and spat, wiped the dangling saliva from her lower lip. She looked south, toward the Marquam Bridge. and saw that a number of small, private yachts and boats were parked at the marina.

Teddy has his own boat. Good place to hide your children.

Too obvious.

Sara approached the center of the Hawthorne Bridge. Cars zipped past her on the rattling, clanging steel-grated deck of the bridge's center. The sound blasted its way into the side of her head, beating against her eardrums. The red paint of the hand railing hadn't been touched in years, worn away by the elements and the passage of time.

Time that slipped faster and faster away as she ran, though it had crawled like molasses back in the Shakespeare Garden.

She stopped at the middle. Doubled over, inhaling through the coffee straws her lungs had become. The breeze was cool and penetrating out over the water as it whipped past, heightening the chill of the soaked running shirt molding itself around her skin. She felt the sun on her back, then straightened up and put her hands behind her head.

Breathe. Breathe. Don't puke. I'm here, you bastard. Where East meets West. What am I supposed to be looking for? Some kind of key?

She looked at the phone in her hand, waiting for it to ring.

Are you supposed to call me? What am I supposed to do?

Sara spun in desperate circles, searching the area around her feet, across the bridge to the other side, up at the towering green trusses. She heard the roar of a hulking metal beast as a TriMet bus slouched its way by, lumbering along, kicking up dust that pelted her skin.

All the other instructions were on a piece of paper.

She twirled, hoping to see a flash of white. Some bit of guidance. Something to point her way to the next level.

I don't see anything. Nothing there. Nothing on the sidewalk. Anything wrapped around the railing? Shit. No. Empty. Is it on me somewhere? Has it been with me this whole time? No pockets in the shirt...no pockets in the shorts...nothing in the key pocket...Shoes? Shoes? Damn. No. Where in the hell is the key?

She walked to the railing and leaned across it, looking for anything below, feeling the sun-warmed metal on her palms. The deep green water of the Willamette swirled along some fifty feet down. The height, coupled with dehydration and exhaustion, caused an overpowering feeling of vertigo. Sara backed away, afraid that she might topple over the edge and plunge into the river. This world, the real one, wasn't like the landscape inside the realm of *Juggernaut*, where you could bump into the outer limits of the backdrop and be stopped from going further. A trip over *this* ledge meant something she didn't want to think about.

Sara looked to her left. A streetlamp reached into the sky and she walked over to it, intending to use the metal post as a support, something to lean against while the dizzy spell passed.

Before she flopped back against it, she saw a small bulge protruding from the front side. She looked closer, and then she gasped. Right at eye level, underneath a wide, clear strip of tape, was a bronze-colored key stuck to the lamppost.

She peeled it away with harried, scrabbling fingers. Ripped the key from the tape's sticky grasp.

The phone rang.

She answered, "I found it, found the key."

"Good for you, Sara. My apologies for the delay. I was having a bit of fun with your children. Who knew they could...*bleed* so easily?"

CHAPTER 9
DJ

DJ sat in a plush leather chair across from Jim Rutherford, the CEO and President of LightPulse Productions. The private office had one glass wall that offered a view of the interior machinations of the company, another was populated with promotional posters of their past releases, and, behind him, a shelved wall held a number of awards and family photographs. The windows to his right were covered with drawn shades, allowing parallel strips of sunlight to penetrate into the room. No overhead lights illuminated the area, and no desk lamps were present to give off a soft glow.

The cave-like atmosphere reminded DJ of some super villain's secret lair.

The desk was as big as a full-sized mattress and oddly empty, except for a single notepad, one pen, and a laptop. DJ expected mountains of paperwork and a ringing phone. At least a nameplate and some kitschy knickknack, like a Newton's Cradle. Instead, the sparseness of the desk gave DJ the impression that this was a man who had little time for distractions. Or, a man who made it a point to eliminate the near-constant interruptions that invariably came with running a busy, growing company like LightPulse. It was an admirable quality—one that DJ wished he had, as well.

Jim wasn't dressed like the average CEO. At least, not the ones that DJ had interacted with before. His buzz-cut salt and pepper hair complimented the plain black t-shirt he was wearing, along with jeans and sneakers that suggested he was a man who dressed however he wanted because he was in charge.

DJ thought, *Dude looks like a poor man's version of Steve Jobs.*

Jim said, "I hope you don't mind sitting in the dark, Detective. It's easier on my eyes. Too many years of working under these damn office lights. They give me headaches."

"How long have you been involved with video games, Mr. Rutherford? I was a huge fan of *Shotgun Shooter* back in the day." DJ knew he should be jumping right into his questions about Sara—he was already way behind on their timeline, after all—but buttering up the man with a miniature ego boost couldn't hurt. Like Barker said, '*Bees with honey, DJ. More bees with honey.*'

"About thirty years. I was on some of the original Atari teams, if you can believe it. So you liked *Shooter*, huh? Wow. Memories. That was back when this was a tiny shop and I was still involved in the actual programming. Blocky pixels, left to right scrolling, 2D worlds. I miss those days. Now we create these 3D masterpieces with nearly the square mileage of Portland for our players to run around in. But hell, it's what they want." Jim crossed his legs, tented his fingertips. "I've been toying with the idea of releasing a 2D throwback for nostalgia's sake, but since Sara lit the fuse under the *Juggernaut* series, we'd get creamed by the media for a stunt like that."

Eh, sounds like regret, but not enough of a motive for kidnapping. "Have you spoken to her today?"

"Not a word. I've been trying to get in touch with her since she left this morning, but she won't answer her phone."

"And you're aware that her children are missing?"

"That's the report I got from her assistant, Shelley. Such a shame. They're sweet kids, and I hope I can help. Do you have any leads yet?"

"We're working on it. How well do you know Sara—I mean, Mrs. Winthrop?"

"We're close. She's a bulldozer sometimes, but she's one of my favorites. I'm sure you can understand that I'm busy as hell trying to run this place, but I try to keep tabs on everyone here, you know. I do my best to get out into the trenches with these guys so they don't think I'm some seagull owner."

"Seagull owner?"

"Flies in, shits on everything, and then leaves."

DJ chuckled. "I think I've known a few of those." He liked the man, had a strong feeling that he wasn't a suspect, and regretted having to ask his next question. "Are you in any way involved in the disappearance of Sara Winthrop's children?" Such a pointed question obviously wouldn't get a positive answer, but it was designed to take Rutherford by surprise in order to gauge his immediate response.

"Definitely not."

The clear, definitive answer, coupled with the body language of a truth-teller, was the response DJ was looking for, in contrast to the dodging, evasive answers, and nervous tics of a person on the front-end of a lie. He asked, "And do you have any idea who might be?"

"Not in the slightest. Like I mentioned, she's an

-74-

asskicker, but around here," he said, motioning toward the glass wall and the open office on the other side, "she's well liked. Respected. Some of the younger kids have a healthy dose of fear of her, but I love that about Sara. She scares the hell out of my son, Teddy, which is sorta funny, to be honest, and frankly I think he does better work because of it. Out there in the real world, though, I'm sorry to say that I don't know what people think. I can't imagine their opinions would be much different. But here in the office, she gets shit done, Detective Johnson, and we'd be lost without her."

"And you don't think that type of demeanor would be enough to create some animosity?"

"Animosity? Of course it's a possibility, but if every poor sap stuck in a cube got pissed off and kidnapped his boss's kids, there wouldn't be any children left."

"True, Mr. Rutherford, but I'm trying to establish a motive. It has to come from somewhere, and an angry employee is an obvious place to start."

"Not with the kids we have working here. They just want to play video games and have fun. Sara's like the—ah, hell, what do they call the older lady who stays at a sorority house?"

"The house mom," DJ answered, which he knew only because his wife Jessica had been an Alpha Phi at the University of Oregon. Her reluctance to leave her home state was the reason he'd said goodbye to Texas. But for her, he would have done anything.

"That's it, the house mom," Jim said. "She's either the house mom or the drill sergeant that you eventually like and respect, even after he's removed his size eleven boot from

-75-

your ass."

DJ knew what he meant. Four years in the Army, two of them spent as an MP, had left him with distinct memories of that exact same boot insertion and removal. He said, "I had one of those. Believe it or not, we exchange Christmas cards. Was Sara ever in the military?"

"Not unless she was in an ROTC program while she was in school, and I don't remember anything like that on her resume. She started working here right after she got out of college and has been killing it since day one. What Sara has," Jim said, "is an inherent strength." He groaned as he stood up, massaging his lower back. He moved with a slight limp over to the window, pried open two shades, and took a long look out into the world beyond.

DJ waited. According to Barker, if you stayed silent long enough, individuals would usually offer more information than if you had asked them something directly. *People want to talk, DJ. Listening is an art. Hearing is biology.*

Still looking out the window, Jim said, "Detective?"

"Yes, sir?"

"What I'm about to tell you—" The blinds snapped shut with a metallic *chink*. "—should be used with some discretion," Jim said. He leaned against his massive expanse of a desk and crossed his arms. "Do whatever you like with it, and I completely understand that you have an investigation to conduct, but I'm asking you to keep this as contained as you can. I feel guilty for saying this, but I have a multi-million dollar business to run, and I can't risk having Sara's authority undermined if—not if, *when*—you find her children and she's able to come back to work."

There it is. There's the ruthless businessman. You're all the same. At least you made it this far.

He said, "I'll do my best, Mr. Rutherford. You've got a business to run, but I've got three missing children to find."

"I'm well aware," Jim said, pausing. He bounced a hanging foot, toe-tapping the air. "I wasn't sure I should bring this up, because I think in absolutes. Ones and zeroes. Something is, or it isn't. This information is pure speculation, got it?"

"Of course."

"I don't know why I'm telling you this." Jim shifted on the desk. Flashed a look at the ceiling, then down at the floor. His bouncing foot moved faster. "Ah, hell, what I'm trying to say is—before Sara's husband disappeared, I had a hunch that he was cheating on her."

DJ rolled his eyes. *Not you, too. The husband, the husband. I'm looking for the kids, damn you.*

"At the Christmas party—why is it always the Christmas party, huh?—anyway, Sara was talking to some of the programmers from out there in The Belly, and in the back of the room, I saw Brian walk in looking like he'd been running around the block, and about thirty seconds later, one of the waitresses came in after him, putting on some fresh lipstick."

DJ said, "Not exactly proof. And I don't see how that has anything to do with the kids being missing."

"No, it probably doesn't. Like I said, pure speculation, but where I was going with that—my mind wanders, Detective. I dream up these crazy ideas. Storylines, right? I mean, that's what I do for a living. I don't want to distract you with dreamed up scenarios, but what if it's Brian? What if he's come back for the kids?"

"It's something we'll take into consideration."

"You're not a fan of the idea, huh?"

"It's not at the top of my list, Mr. Rutherford," he said. Then another Barker-ism popped in his head: '*Acknowledge the possibilities first, but trust the facts later.*' DJ adjusted his tie, fidgeted in his seat, frustrated with the fact that Barker was rarely wrong and was leaning toward the husband-as-culprit scenario, as well. And now Rutherford hinted at the prospect. "Let's say that it *is* the husband, it *is* Brian Winthrop, and he's come back from the dead or wherever he's been, why now? What makes you think that he would come back two years later and kidnap his own children?"

Jim shrugged. "It's a plausible scenario. When we design games here, we weigh the possible against the whimsical, and if the two meet in the middle, we know we have a winner. In Sara's case, that's all I can come up with."

DJ stood, no closer to having any leads than when he'd walked into Jim Rutherford's office fifteen minutes earlier. Regardless of what the Bloodhound's instincts were telling him, he wasn't about to sit there any longer and dream up convoluted schemes with an aging gamer who lived in some fantasy world where an invading alien army could be considered possible.

Whimsical—yes. Possible—not likely. They'd have a better chance of crafting the plotline for a new game with this nonsense than he would of uncovering the truth if he sat here any longer, entertaining these implausible notions. He had children to find, and he'd already wasted enough time on the inane hypothesizing of Barker and the absurd theories of Rutherford.

He said, "I appreciate your time, Mr. Rutherford. Mind if I ask your staff some questions while I'm here?"

"Be my guest. They're on strict deadlines, so please keep that in mind."

"It won't take long. Any suggestions on where to start?"

"Shelley would be your best bet. She's only been here a couple of months, but I'd say she knows Sara better than anyone in the office. Except for me."

DJ thanked him again, and moved for the door. Opened it, then stopped before he left. "One last thing, Mr. Rutherford. I'm sure you've heard it thousands of times, given your profession, but does the phrase, 'Are you ready to play the game?' have any special meaning around here?"

Rutherford's eyes popped open. "How'd you know about that?"

The reaction surprised DJ so much that he didn't have an adequate response ready. He'd tossed the question out almost as an afterthought, never intending to fully discuss that particular aspect of the case. He said, "It's a—it's a lead we're following."

"A lead? Is Teddy a suspect?"

"Your son? No. Why?"

"Did you two talk before you came in to see me?"

"I didn't. Mr. Rutherford, if you know anything—"

"I'm sure he has nothing to do with Sara's kids."

"Does that phrase have anything to do with *him*?"

"He wanted it on the title sequence in *Juggernaut 3*. The staff shot him down, told him it was too mundane. He came crying to me and then pitched a fit when I agreed with them."

DJ took a single step back inside Rutherford's office. He said, "If that's the case, I have some questions for him. Where's his office?"

"He left early this morning, around ten o'clock. Said something about a golf tournament."

"Any idea which one?"

"If I did know, Detective, I'm not sure I'd be willing to offer that information, given the circumstances."

DJ said, "And you know that impeding an investigation is a serious offense?"

"Young man, there are a lot of things I *do* know that I'm sure you don't. Unfortunately for both of us, I have no idea where Teddy might be, golfing or not."

"I'll still be asking around before I go."

Rutherford shooed him away with a dismissive hand. "Good luck."

CHAPTER 10
SARA

...I didn't know they could bleed so easily.

The words clanged around inside her head. Sara bent over the hand railing and vomited a mixture of bile and breakfast into the Willamette. She retched and dry-heaved until nothing was left. Coughing and spitting, she wiped her mouth with her sweaty forearm, and cursed into the phone. "You son of a bitch. If I ever find you, if you touch my children again, I will—"

"You'll what, Sara?"

"—do whatever you've done to them a thousand times over. Do you understand me?"

"But you're there, and I'm here, and you have a game to play."

It came out before she could stop herself, but the anger, the fury inside her had reached the internal temperature of the sun. Reason, and the result of the consequences that would come, provided a gauzy barrier and her words ripped through unhindered. "You can shove this goddamn game up your ass."

"Now, now, Sara. We mustn't let things get out of hand. And by the way—" Another yelp of pain from one of her children—Lacey, this time. "—I told you not to defy me again."

"*Stop!*" she screamed. If it'd been an option, if it'd been offered as an end to the game, an end to her children's torture, she would've backed up, climbed over the railing, and flung herself into the river. "You win, okay? You win."

"We'll find out who wins when the game is over."

"I have the key, just tell me what to do and I'll do it."

"Do you want to ask your question for this round now, or later?"

She wanted to ask now. She wanted to ask Teddy why he had chosen her. Why he had picked her instead of one of the other senior managers that constantly teased him and made fun of his height and called him 'Little One'.

Why did he get her children involved? Why did he have to bind them and torture them? Why not kidnap her? Why not take her, by herself, to some abandoned warehouse where he could do whatever unmentionable things he wanted to do? If he really wanted to get revenge for whatever offenses she had committed, why drag it out with this elaborate game that had so much room for error?

Because he's a cat playing with a mouse right before it eats it. He wants me *to ask now. To make the game harder.*

"Later," she said. "I'll save it."

The disappointed answer of, "Fine," and the long silence that followed confirmed her guess.

She said, "I'm waiting."

"I'm sorry, Sara. I took a moment to feel how soft your son's hair is. It's like gossamer, isn't it?"

Her stomach churned again. She imagined Teddy standing over her son, running his sausage fingers through Jacob's hair. Saw Jacob's tear-streaked face, cringing, trying to move away but unable to because of the tight ropes or rough chains. Rather than screaming more poisonous threats, she rolled her head from side to side, stretching her neck, trying to maintain control. Made a fist, punched the lamppost hard enough for a knuckle to pop.

Think, Sara, think. He's testing you. What's he want? Obedience? Submission?

She clenched her jaw and said, "You're right."

"Soft, blonde gossamer. You may get to feel it again one day."

"Please just tell me what the next level is."

"Such impatience. I expected you to be eager, but this fire in your belly is encouraging. It should serve you well during the first half of Level Two. I like to call it...*Confusion.* Are you ready to play the game?"

"I'm ready."

And you'd better be ready, because if I ever get the chance—

The voice said, "Keep the phone. Keep the key. Continue to the eastern side of the bridge. Take the bike path exit, down to the parking lot under the bridge. Your transportation will be waiting. I'm sure you'll recognize the car. You will be given further instructions. Do you understand?"

"Yes."

"*Wunderbar!* This next level will provide quite the challenge."

Wunderbar? Doesn't Shelley say that all the time? What did she say that meant? Something in German. Wonderful?

"Oh, and Sara?"

"What?"

"You're doing great...Little One."

Little One. It was more than a hint. It was a taunt, saying, 'I want you to know, come and get me.'

Such a deliberate admission. It was enough, so

obvious. She could go to the police, tell them precisely who had her children. But why, why be so blatant?

Because he has your kids. And you have no idea where. He knows you won't risk it. He's in complete control.

Sara paced back and forth as a woman approached, riding a bicycle. She looked like one of the many environmentally conscious commuters around Portland who biked to and from work every day in an attempt to reduce their carbon footprint, even if it was the size of a baby's shoe. Dressed well in a pants-suit, blue backpack clinging to her shoulders, listening to something on her iPod.

I have to fight back. This might be my only chance.

Are you insane? Don't do it, don't do it, don't do it.

Sara made an impulse decision in the few remaining feet before the biker was upon her. She ran, looking back, trying to match the woman's speed.

When they were side by side, the woman flicked at look at her, then refocused on the bike path ahead.

Sara said, "Can you help me?"

The biker removed her right ear bud. "I'm sorry?"

"Can you slow down a little?"

"What's up?" she asked, easing up her pace.

"My phone is dead," Sara said, wheezing, plodding along the hard concrete. "Would you mind making a call for me? Or can I use your phone? It'll only take me a second."

The woman shook her head. "I'm sorry. I can't."

"If you could call for me—I really need help—you don't have to do it now, just when you get a chance."

"That's not—"

"All I need you to do is call Detective Johnson at the police department. Tell him the game is real, and it's Teddy Rutherford at LightPulse."

"I can't do that, Sara."

Sara ran into an invisible wall, screeching to a halt.

Oh no.

The biker pedaled faster, shouting over her shoulder, "That's not how the game is played."

***

Oh no, oh no, oh no.

How many rules had she broken? How many offenses had she committed with that ridiculous, ill-conceived stunt? How long would it take before the woman told Teddy what she'd done? And what would he do to the kids as a result?

Sara sprinted, chasing after the woman for the remaining half of the bridge, but it was a useless waste of energy. She was on a bike, moving too fast, and had gone out of sight by the time Sara reached the opposite shore. She stopped under the overpass.

Stupid, stupid, stupid. What did I do? What did I do? Who else is watching? It could be anyone.

An older couple strolled past, holding hands, laughing. They smiled at her, said hello. Or were they checking on her, making sure she was playing the game as she should? They kept walking, walking, walking. Sara waited on them to reverse their course, follow her. Check in with Teddy, report that she was on schedule. Paranoia billowed in her mind like a gathering thundercloud. Dark and threatening, voluminous, ready to pour down and soak her last remaining sense of composure.

They never looked back. They kept walking, walking, walking.

She wrapped her arms around her body, doubled over, and cried. Wind blew at her back, scattering the teardrops before they reached the concrete. She thought about Brian and the way he had pulled her in close whenever she was sad or having a bad day. Thought about how she used to lay her head on his shoulder, listening to the bass reverberate in his chest as he told her she'd be fine, that he was there for her, and that she had nothing to worry about. If he was still here, would any of this be happening? Would she be at the office right now, answering emails, making calls, reviewing Shelley's latest copywriting masterwork?

Tell me it'll be okay, Brian. Tell me it'll be okay.

She heard the squeal of brakes as a car slowed to a stop beside her.

The driver called out, "Hey, you need some help?"

Sara stood and waved him off. "I'm fine," she lied. "Bad knee. Hurts to run."

"Go see a doctor," he said, pulling away as a honk from another car urged him on.

She remembered Teddy was tracking her with the phone. He'd be able to see that she'd sprinted to the far edge of the Hawthorne and stopped.

Move, Sara. Move before he calls. Move before the son of a bitch hurts the kids again.

She walked, exhausted from the run, exhausted from the spent emotional energy, up to the bike path exit, and then down toward the Eastbank Esplanade.

The white sedan waited for her in the parking lot. The

sight of it gave her a foreboding sense of dread as black as its tinted windows. What waited inside? Who waited inside? The woman from the bicycle? The man who had driven away in her minivan? The person who had dropped him off back at the gardens?

How many are involved? Three? Three at the least?

She scrambled over the fence, stepped around the bushes, and then walked over to the white sedan. Hesitated at the rear door, yanked it open. Climbed inside. The soft *shunk* of rubber on rubber as the door sealed shut was as loud as a prison cell clanging shut.

The interior of the car was dark from the window tint. Front and rear seats separated by a metal grating, like a police cruiser. The air was thick and difficult to breathe, permeated by the scent of stale cigarette smoke and the lemon-shaped air freshener that dangled from the rear view mirror. The driver, a male, wore a baseball cap pulled low, wraparound shades, and a jacket with the collar up, revealing nothing more than a sliver of his tanned cheek and the pointy tip of his nose.

To her left sat a small, brown paper bag. "Is that for me?"

The driver offered one slow nod.

Sara placed the bag in her lap, almost afraid to open it, but she relented. Inside was a bottle of water, an apple, a small box, and a familiar white slip of paper. She pulled it out and read:

KEYS OPEN LOCKS. LOCKS OPEN CAGES.
24 HOURS. IF YOU THINK HARD, THE ANSWER
WILL COME.

Confusion. I'm supposed to lock myself up for twenty-four hours. What am I supposed to think about for twenty-four hours? And the kids? Just sitting there waiting for me. I'm so sorry, guys. So sorry that Mommy got you into this.

The driver started the car. Drove out of the lot.

Sara reached into the bag and removed the small, square container, examining it as they pulled onto the street, heading east. Charcoal gray, hinged on the back side. A jewelry box. She held it up to her ear and shook. Something rattled inside.

She held her fingers to the lid, waiting, not knowing what to expect. Perhaps some clue, something to help her remember, something to remind her of what she was supposed to think about for the next twenty-four hours.

Twenty-four hours. It seemed impossible. Undoable. But that was what he wanted. The torture of being helpless. The torture of making her sit idly, locked in a cage, unable to do anything. Waiting, waiting, waiting while he controlled the game, controlled her fate, controlled her children's fates. How afraid they must be without their mother, hoping she would save them soon, not knowing why they were trapped in a room with a stranger, not knowing why she hadn't come yet.

The guilt was settling in already, and she wasn't even inside the cage yet.

She looked down at the box, her hands poised, ready to open it.

Did you take this from my house, too, Teddy? What did you find in there to torture me with?

She squeezed, pried the lid back, then slammed it shut when she saw the object inside.

CHAPTER 11
DJ

DJ marched out of Jim Rutherford's office.

What had started out as a pleasant, helpful conversation had disintegrated into a muddled mess, turning his mood foul. But it left him with two leads. The husband theory had its structure built on sand and speculation, while Rutherford's son, Teddy, had just become the prime suspect. The exact phrase match, coupled with his convenient disappearance to an unknown golf tournament, was enough to pursue.

Yet it wasn't as concrete as he would've liked, because it was missing motive, and he wanted a measure of reassurance before he issued an APB for the guy and brought him in for questioning. He didn't want to risk a lawsuit if Teddy Rutherford were standing on the 18th fairway over at Riverside or Heron Lakes.

He called the station, asked them to check up on golf tournaments in the area. "Call me if you find any. Call me faster if you don't."

DJ approached the nearest employee, a scrappy looking kid with a greasy, unwashed mop and pimpled skin. He went into Barker's version of 'steamroller mode': a tactic he used to overpower and intimidate someone that might offer more information when confronted with a bigger presence. *Bees with honey, DJ, but piss and vinegar when necessary.*

DJ said, "Name and rank, soldier."

The kid looked up from his laptop. "I'm sorry?"

"I said name and rank, soldier."

"My rank?"

Doesn't work on the clueless, Barker. He said, "Forget it. What's your name?"

"Jeremy. And you're…?"

"Detective Johnson," he said, flashing his badge. "Where can I find Sara Winthrop's assistant?"

Jeremy recoiled. He gave a simple, "Whoa," and added, "Not sure. I think she's gone for the day."

"Gone?"

"Yeah. Pretty sure."

"How sure is pretty sure?"

"Well, I mean, very, I guess."

"You guess?"

He pointed toward the front door. "I heard her tell somebody over there that she'd see them tomorrow."

"You *heard?* Did you actually *see* her leave?"

"Kinda."

"Kinda?" *What's he hiding?* "Come on, you either did or you didn't—which is it?"

"I did."

"And you're positive?"

"Positive," Jeremy said, and then added with some reluctance, "She's got a tight body. I checked out her ass when she left. So yes, I saw her leave. You got me. Guilty as charged."

Jesus. He's just embarrassed. "Not exactly a crime, Skippy. When was this?"

"Ten-ish," he said, pausing to think. "Wait, yeah, ten o'clock. She and Teddy both left right before the group meeting."

DJ put his hands on his hips, examined him for any signs of malfeasance. No twitching, no avoided eye contact, no hint of deception in his body language. He seemed legit. A goofy dork who happened to be admiring an untouchable ass from a distance. Right place, right time.

So the girl who knows the most about Sara and the guy who has a connection to the note are both gone, and they left around the same time. Coincidence?

Jeremy said, "Anything else? I'm kinda behind here, dude."

"You said you heard her say she'd see somebody tomorrow? Any idea who she was talking to?"

"There's like, forty-five people here. Best guess would be Sara."

DJ sighed. "Not likely." Dead end. Not that observant when he wasn't checking out somebody's ass. "What do you know about Mrs. Winthrop?"

"Is she in trouble?"

"Not with us. How would you describe her?"

Jeremy thought for a second, said, "About five-eight. Brown hair, brown eyes—"

"Not physically. Her personality. She get along with people here? Any reason to think someone might hold a grudge?"

"Not that I know of. She's kinda like a bowl of ice cream. Cold but sweet at the same time."

"A bowl of ice cream, huh? You come up with that all by yourself?"

"I write some of the creative storylines for our games. Keeps me thinking in metaphors."

"Sounds like a fun job. And Teddy Rutherford? What

kind of dessert is he?"

"Um...a sugar cookie?"

"How so?"

Jeremy looked around, wary of prying ears. "Promise you won't tell him I said this?"

"Promise."

With a hint of a smile, he said, "He *thinks* he's delicious, but in reality, he's just small and boring."

***

DJ drove away from LightPulse, wondering where he should go next. Maybe catch up with Barker, see if he had gotten anything solid from the witnesses at the Rose Gardens, let him know about Teddy Rutherford and the absent assistant. Question Sara's friends and neighbors, which they should've been doing hours ago, instead of wasting precious minutes on half-cocked theories about Brian Winthrop.

Damn. We're blowing this one. Big time.

The remainder of his conversations with some of the other employees proved to be as insignificant as Jeremy's sugar cookie. The general impression of Sara around the office was exactly as Jim Rutherford had described. She was fierce but encouraging, down to earth but revered. They had witnessed her heated encounters with Teddy, but it was nothing more than putting him in his place, like the rest of their management did on a daily basis.

The ones that had interacted with her outside the office talked about how great she was with her children and how well she'd coped when her husband disappeared. DJ sensed that the hat she wore at LightPulse was completely different than the one she wore at home, which wasn't unusual for anyone juggling a high-profile career and family life.

And from what he got based on their answers, Teddy was universally disliked around the office but either knew and didn't care, or floated along in this oblivious state of being God's gift to humanity. A Napoleon complex wasn't enough to make the guy a suspect, but his connection to Sara's note and the timing of his absence was, and it was close enough to make DJ suspicious.

But what about his dad? He knew where the phrase came from. Is he involved?

Jim Rutherford was a remote possibility, but he had too much to lose and too little to gain from kidnapping the children of his shining star.

"Don't chase, DJ," he said. "Stay focused."

His cell rang. He whipped into the nearest parking lot, stopped and answered. "Johnson."

"Got some info on those golf tournaments, JonJon."

"Seriously, Davis? You, too?"

A chuckle, followed by, "Too easy, DJ. Couldn't resist."

"Whatever. The tournaments?"

"Bupkis. None scheduled until the weekend."

That's a game-changer. "What do you have on Teddy Rutherford?" he asked, then spelled out the last name for clarification.

"Hold on a sec."

DJ heard the clacking of a keyboard as Sergeant Davis pulled up the information. While he waited, he asked,

"Barker check in yet?"

"Yep. Said he tried your cell. Wants you to call him ASAP. Okay...Theodore Alan Rutherford, last known address...1848 Graystone. Wow. Guy must have a gold-plated toilet seat."

"Any priors?"

"Two. Nothing major. One speeding ticket and one assault, six years ago. Looks like it might've been a bar fight."

"Send a car over to his house."

"Want us to bring him in?"

The phrase match, no golf tournaments. It was the best he had. "If he's there. If not, start looking."

He called Barker next.

Barker answered with a perturbed, "Where the hell have you been?"

"LightPulse. Asking around. I think we may have something."

"Good. I didn't come up with much here. Some of the witnesses said they saw a naked woman. Said she threw on some clothes and hightailed it down the hill."

"On foot?"

"Like she was in a big damn hurry to get somewhere. But hell, who wouldn't be if they'd been standing around naked in front of a hundred strangers?"

"Right. Sara left the school in a hybrid Sienna. Beige, I think. Any sign of it?"

"Damn, cowboy, you might've mentioned that. Had a lady tell me she recognized the naked woman from the parking lot. Light brown minivan, she said, but it ain't there now. Not where she said it was."

"If she left on foot and didn't come back to get it, where'd it go?"

"Better yet, who took it?"

"Get somebody on it, then meet me at 1848 Graystone. Davis has somebody on the way, but I think you and I need to go have a look."

"Residential? You got a possible?"

"Heavy on the possible, but no motive yet."

"Anything to do with the husband?"

No, Barker. Jesus, would you give it up?

"Negative. Teddy Rutherford, son of the LightPulse CEO. See you in fifteen. I'll explain later."

***

By the time DJ got to Teddy Rutherford's home near Portland Heights, Barker was already waiting on him, leaning on the side of his car, admiring the house from a distance. DJ parked behind him.

Barker whistled as he walked up. "What do you think? Million five? How do people afford this shit?"

"Spending his daddy's dollars certainly doesn't hurt." DJ looked up to the house, taking in the spectacle. His shoebox-sized home could easily fit inside three times. Modern design with lots of straight lines and boxy edges. Gray exterior with white trim. A cobblestone walkway led up to a sky blue door. Lush, vibrant landscaping made it look like the house was hiding within a jungle rather than being a place where a person might lay his head down at night. A huge, three-paneled picture window took up a good portion of the left side of the facing wall, and on the opposite side of the front door, a smattering of rectangular windows formed a wavelike pattern.

Barker said, "I get dizzy looking at it. Makes me think of those flashing cartoons that give kids seizures. Would you live in something like this?"

"If I had *your* salary, I might."

"My salary couldn't rent a room in that thing, cowboy." He angled sideways to face DJ. "What's the deal here? Uniforms left about five minutes ago. Nobody home."

"Damn. It's never easy, is it?"

"You'll learn one of these days."

"And I'm sure you'll take credit for it when I do."

DJ recounted the details of his LightPulse visit. The shitty meeting with Jim Rutherford. The connection to Teddy and the note. The golf tournament. The *lack* of golf tournaments. The unaccounted for assistant and her coincidental departure. The teasing that Teddy Rutherford may or may not have taken offense to. "The lead is there," he said, "but I don't feel like it's enough for motive."

Barker said, "What we feel and what we can reason—"

"'*Do not sleep in the same bed together.*' I know, Barker. I know."

"I wish you'd stop interrupting me."

"I don't need to. Your ramblings are ground into my brain."

"One of these days I might surprise you with something you've never heard before."

"When you do, I'll be all ears."

Barker tapped a cigarette out of his soft pack. Lit it with a one-handed *click* and strike of his Zippo, then took a long drag, slowly exhaling, letting the billowing smoke get lost in the breeze. "What now, cowboy? We've got a missing woman, her missing children, a missing husband, a missing suspect, a missing assistant."

"Don't forget the missing babysitter. The Bluesong woman."

"Seems to me like we're doing the exact opposite of our jobs. Losing people instead of finding them. I'm not sure I've ever gone this far in the wrong direction."

DJ decided against reminding his partner of all the time they'd wasted that morning chasing puffs of smoke that dissipated faster than the filth coming out of his lungs. "We're here. We might as well take a look around."

Barker stood quietly, smoking his cigarette, staring at the house.

"Well?" DJ said.

"Hold your horses. I'm pondering."

"Pondering what, Barker? We have to do—" DJ stopped mid-sentence as the front door swung open.

The young woman that stumbled out of the doorway and lurched toward them was naked from the waist down, with one strap of white cloth around her left wrist and one on her right ankle. Ripped purple t-shirt. What looked to be a ball gag dangled like a sadistic necklace. Her legs were covered in cuts and bruises that were so prominent, DJ could see them and her black eye from fifteen yards away.

Barker choked on his cigarette smoke, coughed hard.

DJ said, "Holy shit." He sprinted toward her, shouting back, "Call 9-1-1, Barker. Now!"

"Help me," she said, and then collapsed on the walkway.

CHAPTER 12
SARA

Sara opened the small box again as the driver headed east in the direction of Gresham and Powell Valley. She had to be sure that what she saw wasn't a trick of her imagination. Could it be the exhaustion? Was she hallucinating? It was possible. She was empty. Physically to the point of collapsing. Mentally to the point of seeing things that just couldn't be.

The object inside was a relic of history come to life. It was a memory that had manifested itself into a tangible form. It was the dead rising.

Sara peered inside and immediately regretted looking. It sat motionless, right where it was thirty seconds earlier, daring her to pick it up and *feel* what was really there.

Brian's wedding ring. It's not possible.

She reached into the box and pinched the ring, pulled it out and examined it in the light. The thick band of hammered tungsten felt cool on her fingertips. The tinted windows made it harder to see, but it *looked* like Brian's. She held it by the outside, tilting it this way and that until she was able to get a better glimpse of the interior. She didn't want it to be true, but it was.

The inscription read:

Forever Yours – SLW

A storm surge of emotions—anger and frustration and

hope—rushed over her body, plowing their way through like a ten-foot-high wall of water over shoreline streets. It tore what remained of her stability to splinters, ripping it from the foundation, grinding it into shards of unrecognizable flotsam before it retreated and dragged her sanity with it.

She inhaled as deep as her constricted lungs would allow and let loose a banshee scream toward the front of the car. The driver ducked and swerved. She pounded the metal grating between them with her fists, rattling the cage. She wrapped her fingers through the holes and shook and shook and shook, pulling and pulling, trying to rip it free so she could claw at the driver's eyes, wrap her fingers around his neck until he couldn't breathe, or reach inside his chest and rip out his beating heart.

When he didn't turn around, when he didn't acknowledge her, when he did nothing more than click on his blinker to make a left turn, it unleashed a level of fury so deep that Sara began to feel cramps forming in the arches of her feet. She screamed. She raged. She pounded the metal grating until her knuckles bled. She shouted, "Who are you? Why are you doing this? Where did you get my husband's ring?"

On and on she went, screaming every question she could think of, every question that had plagued her since early that morning. She knew her temper tantrum that had escalated into a full-bore Hiroshima explosion was against whatever rules Teddy had dreamed up, but she was past containing herself. All the emotions she'd swallowed and hidden away for the past two years, all the anxiety and stress and fear that she'd kept buried so the kids wouldn't see, everything, all of it, detonated there in that car, leveling the walls she'd built around her psyche.

Sara screamed until her throat was raw and her vocal chords burned. Every muscle in her body ached from the vehement expulsion of her wrath and she went limp, flopping back onto the seat when no more words would come.

She looked down at Brian's ring in her open palm. The aftershocks of pain sent tremors vibrating through her hand and she could feel her pulse throbbing through the fluid in her swollen knuckles.

What did you do to him?

She tried one last time with the driver, this stoic courier delivering his pathetic, distraught package. "Where did Teddy find this?"

Nothing.

So many questions. No answers. Did the ring mean that Brian was still alive? Or worse, did it mean the opposite? What possible link could there be between Teddy and Brian?

Her chauffeur, the stone statue in the front seat, pulled over to the side. Sara sat up straight, tried to figure out where they were, but didn't recognize the area. Somewhere east of Portland proper, but not quite to Gresham yet. The driver reached up and worked a green strip of cloth through one of the openings in the grate.

"What's that for?"

His one word response was, "Blindfold."

Indignant, she said, "I'm not wearing that."

"Blindfold."

"No."

"Blindfold."

She clenched her jaws. "I said no."

The driver reached down, grabbed something from the seat beside him. He held up what was left of Jacob's Tyrannosaurus Rex t-shirt, the one he'd worn to school that morning. The one he'd worn so much the color had begun to fade. "Blindfold."

"If you hurt him—"

"Blindfold."

She ripped the green strip of fabric from its metal grasp. "If you've done something to him or my girls...if I get out of this goddamn game alive, and if I ever, *ever* find out who you are, you better pray to God there's another wall between us, because I'll be coming for you. Do you understand me?"

"Blindfold."

Sara wrapped the cloth around her head, covering her eyes, turning out the lights on a world that was already dark. She shifted the material around until she found a thinning spot on the old t-shirt, allowing her just enough sight to make out shapes in the sunlight.

What good will it do me? "Done," she said.

She heard him shuffling around, heard the familiar clicking of fingers on a keypad. Silence. More clicking.

"What're you doing? Did you hear me? I said I'm done."

The car began to move again. The driver turned on the radio. Classical music blared from the speakers, drowning out every other sound.

I can't hear where we're going, asshole. The blindfold is enough.

But with limited sight, her other senses took over,

amplified themselves. She felt the rough material of the car's seat on the back of her legs. The throbbing in her swollen hands. The weight of the key in one, and the ring in the other. She felt the vibration of the tires rolling across decaying roads. Every pothole felt like they were falling. Every incline, a roller coaster climbing toward its apex. Tasted the remnants of vomit. She remembered the apple and bottle of water.

Save it. Might be all you'll get.

I hope they're feeding the kids. They didn't eat much this morning. Oh God, why didn't I make them finish their breakfast? Why didn't I, why didn't I, why didn't I?

Breathe...breathe...breathe...

Everything will be fine, everything will be fine, everything will be fine.

Sara repeated the mantra in her mind, even said it aloud a number of times, but it didn't help. No matter how much she tried to convince herself that the ending of the game would be a happy one, no matter how many alternate ending scenarios that she came up with, the feeling that something bad would happen wouldn't go away.

Sliding into depression was an understatement. She careened downward, headlong, toward the awaiting and inevitable bottom. Thought about how rare truly happy endings were out in the real world. You got handed the results and you had to acknowledge them and move on, regardless of the outcome or circumstances.

***

She had no idea how long they'd been driving. Twenty

minutes? Half an hour? Surely they were out of the city, but for all she knew, they could've doubled back. It was too hard to make out where they'd gone with the fleeting glimpses through the material, but it wasn't worth risking a peek. If the driver saw her do it, one call to Teddy might result in more pain for her children.

As the car rattled and bounced along, Sara got the feeling that they were no longer on a paved road. The vibrations were different. More rugged and unforgiving. Wherever he was taking her, and however long it had been, it was far from where she wanted to be.

Which was on her porch, in her rocking chair, watching the kids play a game of freeze tag in their postage stamp of a backyard. Or in their living room, putting together a puzzle after dinner. Lying between the twins, reading them a bedtime story as her little boy dozed across the hall, mouth open, slobbering on his favorite pillow.

We just did that yesterday. Seems like a year ago. I miss them so much.

She slipped Brian's ring over her left thumb.

I miss you too, sweetheart. What happened that day? Where did you go? How did Teddy get your ring?

The radio went silent. The driver made a lurching left turn that slung Sara sideways and then he slammed on the brakes, pitching her forward into the grating. Without the benefit of vision, it was impossible to tell when she needed to brace herself.

"Ouch," she said, rubbing the impact spot on her forehead. "How about a little warning, asshole?"

"Sorry," he said, shutting off the car.

"Did you just apologize to me?"

"Yes."

"Why?"

Five seconds passed. Ten. He shifted in the front seat. Fingers tapped on the steering wheel. Not being able to see his reaction unnerved her.

He said, "Guilt."

"Guilt? Guilt for the knot on my head or guilt for what you're doing?"

"Both."

"So you *are* human."

Another long silence, then a dejected, "Sometimes."

With her heightened sense of hearing, Sara picked up on the regret in his tone. She wondered if nudging it along would help. She needed an ally. "Why're you doing this?"

"Because."

"Because? *Because?* What kind of answer is that? What if it were your children? Do you have kids?"

Tap, tap, tapping on the steering wheel. "One."

"Honestly? And you're doing this to me?"

"Sorry," he said. It came out laced with frustration, and she didn't want to push him too far in the wrong direction.

"Boy or girl?" she asked.

"Boy."

"How old?"

"Eight."

"It's a good age. I remember when my girls were eight. We had so much fun together playing dress up and watching Disney together. They're twins, though. Quite a handful. My son, he's five. Typical boy, you know? Dirt and lizards and monster trucks. What's your son's na—"

"Quiet."

She was getting through. She could feel it.

Delicate, Sara. Don't go too far. Push too hard and he'll turn on you.

She said, "It's okay. You don't have to tell me. I don't need to know." She leaned forward, softened her voice. "Aren't little boys the best? What's your favorite thing about him?"

"Smile."

"Don't you love that mischievous grin they get? Mine has the cutest dimples. And he has this thing he does—"

"Enough," the driver said.

Sara heard his car door open and the warning chime of the keys in the ignition. "Wait," she said. "I'm sorry. Don't—"

Her door opened and then a rough, gloved hand wrapped around her upper arm. He squeezed, hard, dragging her out of the car. He was strong, and for an instant she was airborne before she hit the ground, face-first, getting a mouthful of dirt, busting her bottom lip on a rock. She spat out a mixture of earth and blood. She tried to get to her feet, felt a foot on her ribs, shoving her back down.

"Stay," he said.

She complied, rolled onto her back, hands up in submission.

She listened to him walk away, heard both car doors slam shut, and then receding footsteps.

I can run.

You have no idea where you are. He has a car. You'll never make it.

And Teddy might punish the kids.

Might?

Sara ran her tongue across her lip, felt the swelling. More blood leaked into her mouth. She swallowed, afraid to move. Afraid he would hurt her if she disobeyed.

The sun warmed her face, and from above came the sounds of rustling leaves as the trees creaked and swayed in the wind. Somewhere nearby, a stream crawled its way across some rocks. A bird chirped.

You went too far. You had him.

He said he felt guilty.

Guilt can turn on you.

She heard the approaching sounds of heavy boots on gravel. She lay still.

What if I surprised him? Kicked the bastard in the nuts?

Then what? What if he has a gun? If you're dead, what happens then?

What if I got the gun from him? Forced him to take me to the kids?

He may not know where they are. Bad, bad idea. Too many things could go wrong.

I can do it. I'm sure I—

Her scheming ended when felt a hand in her hair, tugging her up from the ground. It hurt, but she refused to scream, refused to show any more signs of pain.

Sara heard what sounded like the crackling of a paper bag, then felt him shove it into her hand.

"Go," he said, whipping her around, shoving at her back.

He led her along, tightening the grip on her upper arm. She tripped over something, felt like a root, and he lifted her upright. They trudged downhill, then up again, tree limbs scraping her skin. A ragged, broken limb gouged a chunk out of her thigh. Blood trickled down her leg.

"Faster," he said.

The voice rained down from above, miles and miles above her head. She tried to remember how tall the guy was at the Rose Gardens, the one who had taken her van. She had no way of knowing until he removed the blindfold, but her sixth sense *felt* that he was the same man.

Tall. Dark hair. Blue eyes.

The thought sparked a memory from earlier in the day.

The guy. The guy, the guy, the guy. The tall one in the grocery store? Was he following me? Was that why he was checking me out?

Should I ask if that was him? Throw him off? He won't expect me to remember.

He pulled her to the right, leading her in a different direction. She took a chance, saying, "It's such a shame."

"What?"

"You seemed nice in the grocery store."

He didn't respond, but the faint, halting hitch in his step was enough.

CHAPTER 13
DJ

DJ and Barker stood in front of the Rutherford home, watching the paramedics load the young woman into the back of the ambulance. They drove away with instructions for the doctor to call as soon as she was stable and coherent. DJ had tried to talk to her while Barker was inside, tried to ask her what had happened, but her delusional ramblings had made no sense.

He said, "I don't know, Barker. She was out of it. Kept saying something about how this woman told her she'd be okay."

"A *woman*?"

"She kept repeating, 'She said I'd be okay.' Over and over. *She* said she'd be okay. Nothing about a *he*. Nothing about Rutherford."

"And?"

"And what, Barker? You don't find that strange?"

"That I do, cowboy, but from the looks of her, I doubt that girl could tell you what day it is."

"Doesn't make any sense, that's all I'm saying. You find anything in the house?"

"Possible signs of forced entry on the back door. Single chair down in the basement. I figure that's where she was being kept. Managed to get herself loose. Other than that, the place is clean. Nothing like a weird torture room or crazy sex toys. From the looks of it, dude has more money to spend than he has sense. You should've seen the size of the boob tube."

"Forced entry on the back door, you said?"

"Wasn't much. Closed. Not locked, but it didn't look like somebody beat it in with a sledgehammer. More like it'd been pried open with a screwdriver. Figured Dumbo locked himself out at some point."

DJ looked at the house. Something didn't feel right. "What're we missing here? Where's the disconnect?"

"The disconnect?"

"We got a suspect in one kidnapping keeping another vic in his basement," DJ said. He pinched his earlobe, thinking. "But then there's a possible forced entry and the girl mentioning a *she*."

Barker studied him. "I ain't following."

"What if she was planted here?"

Barker laughed. "God almighty, DJ. And you say I come up with some cockamamie ideas."

"I'm assuming you've heard of the word 'hypothetical' before."

"Look here, cowboy, when I say explore the possibilities, I don't mean for you to put Elmore Leonard to shame with your plotlines."

"Then what's your theory?"

"Whoever *she* is," Barker said, "she partnered up with Rutherford. Conned our vic with some sweet words, brought her back here."

"Still doesn't feel right."

"Occam's Razor. Simplest explanation."

DJ put his hands behind his head. "Say we disregard my left field idea, make it a non-factor for now...if Rutherford and this mystery woman are working together, there has to be at least a third person, maybe more, right? He was at the LightPulse office until ten o'clock, and the Winthrop kids went missing around nine at separate locations. So while he was at the office, the rest of his team was out doing his dirty work."

"Now you're getting somewhere. And who knows how long that poor gal was down in the basement."

"But why, though? We don't have a ransom note. We've got a random woman in her twenties and three kids of a coworker. What're they doing?"

"I told you earlier we were dealing with a sociopath. Now it might be two. And if they ain't trying to ransom, what they're doing," Barker said, "is collecting trophies."

Trophies, DJ thought. *That would tie in with the idea of making Sara play a game.*

"Horseshoes and hand grenades, but it's all we've got," he said. "And I hate to ask, but where's the husband in all this? You give up on him?"

Barker shook his head. "Not yet. If he ain't the main course, he's a side dish."

"You think he could be the third?"

"Hell, I've seen stranger things. C'mon, let's get back to the station, see if that young lady was reported. Hospital might have an ID on her by the time we get back, and if there's a connection between her and Mrs. Winthrop or Captain Ugly House here, we'll get a better lead on the kids."

***

DJ found Barker coming out of the bathroom, tucking

in his shirt. He said, "Hospital got an ID on the girl. Anna Townsend," and handed over her thin file. "Woke up long enough to give a name and then passed back out."

"Can we go talk to her?"

"Doc said to give it a couple of hours."

"What's her story?"

"Anna Townsend...also known as Stardust."

"Stardust?" Barker asked, flipping the folder open. "She a stripper?"

"Works the poles at this new club called Ladyfingers."

"Heard of it. Never been."

"Sure," DJ said, dragging the word out.

Barker ignored him. "What do we got here...one prior...driving under the influence. Twenty-one years old. Let me guess, paying for college?"

"Nope. Not your average stereotype. Get this...according to her *husband*, they're happily married with a one-year-old son."

"No shit? They got an open relationship or something?"

"Sounded as secure as Fort Knox. High school sweethearts. Said she started stripping to help pay the bills once he lost his job. Money is too good for her to quit, so he's a stay-at-home dad."

"I'll be damned. So why didn't he report her missing?"

"I had to pry it out, but he said that she doesn't get off work until around three in the morning. Once in a while, if some guy flashes big dollars, she'll go home with him for a private show. No sex, just extra money, and she'll get back around six or seven. He was worried because she wasn't answering her cell, but knew we wouldn't do anything until she'd been gone for twenty-four hours."

Barker pushed his glasses up to his forehead, rubbed the bridge of his nose. "I'm spitballing here, but I doubt there'll be a link between a stripper and Mrs. Winthrop."

"But," DJ said, "a stripper and a guy with money—that's a no-brainer."

"Let's go have a Q and A. One of the other girls might be able to give us some info on where she went last night."

DJ agreed, but couldn't escape the feeling that they were getting further and further away from Sara's children, regardless of whether or not they were heading in the right direction by chasing down Teddy Rutherford and his mystery-woman partner.

It keeps getting deeper and deeper, he thought.

Twenty minutes later, they walked into the Ladyfingers Gentleman's Club, Portland's latest addition to the growing cadre of strip joints that gave the city a higher per capita rate of naked dancer locations than Sin City itself. Some were prominent and popular; others were tucked away on side streets with little more than pink neon signs promising *LIVE NUDE GIRLS*. The market had yet to saturate, and doubtfully never would. If the world ran out of men (and women) willing to pay for the chance to see a woman in her birthday suit, it would be the end of times.

DJ had only been a paying customer once, a couple years back, for a friend's bachelor party. The experience was awkward. He'd found it difficult to look them in the eye, difficult to stare at the parts he was supposed to be looking at, difficult to figure out what to do with his hands during a private dance that had set him back fifty bucks.

He and Barker had been a couple of times for on-the-job visits and it was easier to feel in control and not under the spell the strippers seemed to cast over every person desperately waving a single, hoping to get a closer glimpse.

And Ladyfingers was even more acceptable when the doors had just been unlocked and the stages were empty.

They stopped a couple of feet inside the doorway. No patrons yet, no bartender, no girls.

The same smell that came with every strip club hung in the air. Evaporated alcohol, girl sweat, and cheap perfume. It was thick and cloying. DJ knew it would get stuck in his clothes and made him think about having to do laundry. He glanced around at the dark walls, the mirrors, the strobe lights hanging overhead. Rows of liquor bottles stood at attention behind the bar. Across from it, the main stage perched three feet above the floor with a signature, shiny pole in the middle. Tables and chairs stretched all the way to the back of the room where two smaller stages occupied each side.

He said, "I still haven't figured out why these damn places make me so uncomfortable."

"It's because you're not human," Barker said.

"True, but at least I don't put dinner on the table for half the strippers in town."

"The ex ain't coming back, and I'm not getting any better looking, JonJon."

"I know it used to take months to paint a naked woman back in your day, but you've heard of the internet, right?"

Barker examined him, head to toe, squinting at DJ's face, at his ear.

"What're you doing?" DJ asked.

"Looking for your mute button."

A bartender emerged from the swinging doors to their left, her tattooed arms straining to hold onto the three cases of beer. She noticed them, said, "No tits for another hour, guys. Can I get you a drink?" She lifted the beer cases up, sat them down heavily on the bar. The bottles clinked around inside.

DJ and Barker walked over, showed their badges. Barker said, "No thank you, ma'am. On duty. Detectives Barker and Johnson."

She said, "And the cherry is popped."

"The cherry?" DJ said.

"Been open a month. You're not the first cops we've had in here, but you're the first that were on duty." She opened one of the cases and began restocking the cooler.

Barker said, "I'm sure we won't be the last, either. Mind if I ask your name?"

"Mildred," she said, tearing open another box.

"Is that right? That purple mohawk don't exactly scream such an old fashioned name."

"Blame my grandmother."

Barker chuckled. "Don't be ashamed of it. My dear ol' gran was a Mildred, too."

DJ shot a quick look at him, wondered if he was lying. Remembered Barker saying, '*Butter can go on both sides of the toast, cowboy.*'

Mildred finished up the third box, leaned over the bar toward them. "Not trying to be a douche, but I got shit to do, man. What's up?"

DJ said, "You have a dancer here who goes by Stardust?"

"Anna. She's a good one."

"And were you working last night?"

"I own the place, Detective. I'm here every night. Something happen to her?"

Barker said, "*Something* happened, but we'd like to find out what."

"Oh, shit. She's not dead, is she?" Mildred stood up straight, looking from Barker to DJ, Barker to DJ.

"She's alive, but she won't be back to work for some time," Barker said.

DJ asked, "Did you know she was going home with customers after hours? Doing private shows?"

"It's against my rules, but some of the girls do it. I can't stop whatever happens once their shifts are over."

"Was Mrs. Townsend paying extra attention to anyone in here last night? Short guy, about this tall. Probably flashing bills with a couple extra zeros."

"She was," Mildred said. "But not a dude. Some girl. They were down at the end of the bar, flirting with each other for half the night."

DJ waffled his curious glance between Barker and Mildred. "Can you describe her?"

"Straight brown hair, shoulder length. Great smile. Nice body. At least what I saw of it. I remember thinking that if she threw on a bunch of makeup and some glitter, she could go onstage."

"Any chance she paid with a credit card?"

"Nah. She had two Cosmos, paid cash for both."

"Good memory," Barker said.

Mildred picked up a rag, swiped at some crumbs. "It's what we do. You work behind a bar long enough, you learn to pay attention to the big tippers."

"Can you think of anything out of the ordinary about her?" DJ asked. "Anything we could identify her with? Tattoos, unusual birthmarks?"

"Um...no, just naturally pretty. Around the same age as Anna. Low-cut blouse. Good rack, like she'd had them done, you know?" She focused on the countertop like she was staring into her memory. "Other than that...oh yeah, a necklace with these diamonds that looked like two letters sort of intertwined together. Might've been initials."

DJ said, "You remember that?"

"With cleavage like hers, who wouldn't be looking right there?"

Barker said, "Can you remember what they were?"

"My memory's not *that* good."

"Take a guess," DJ said. "Anything helps."

"Shit...okay...*D*. I'd say one of them was a *D*."

Barker said, "One last question, Miss Mildred. Did Anna leave with her?"

"She was here until around two-thirty. Anna left a few minutes past three. After that, who knows?"

"Thanks for your time," Barker said. "Might see you again one of these days."

"First drink is on the house."

Back on the sidewalk, heading for Barker's car, DJ said, "How many boxes of Cracker Jacks do we have to open before there's a *good* prize inside?"

"Preaching to the choir, DJ. Preaching to the choir. Now hit that mute button I was looking for. The Bloodhound here needs to think a minute."

They walked the last two blocks in silence.

Downtown Portland could get hot and crowded in the middle of summer with so many people walking and shopping, sitting outside to eat. These days, it seemed like any shop with a front door and a couple of chairs handy would set up a table and offer something *al fresco*. A cup of coffee, a scone, a glass of wine and some cheese. It was fun when he and Jessica actually had a chance to get downtown and pass a lazy Saturday together, but when he was in a hurry and on a mission to get somewhere with no destination, navigating the window-shopping horde was a nightmare.

Jesus, it's three o'clock on a Tuesday. Why are you people not at work?

He needed to talk, needed to get his mind off the crowds and the people in his way before he started shoving somebody. He said, "We can peg both of them back there between 2:30 and 3:00. Confirms the *she* that Anna was talking about. I don't think we got much else out of that, do you?"

"Not a whole lot, but don't forget, today's suspect was brought to you by the letter *D*."

DJ was already tense and the possibility of Barker chasing another set of empty leads ratcheted his agitation higher. He threw his hands into the air. "Barker, that could've been anything," he said. "Bigger net, bigger waste."

"I wouldn't say it was *entirely* a waste. I might get a free drink out of it."

"Would you stop for a minute? Seriously. We're blowing this whole freaking thing. We got more questions being thrown at us than Alex Trebek, and you're happy about a free drink? Where's Teddy Rutherford? Who's the mystery woman? Where's Sara Winthrop?"

Barker said, "They're all having drinks together, laughing at a couple of dumbass cops."

"You're kidding, right?"

"I'm just saying—"

"Rein it in, man. You're chasing. Forget the necklace, forget the husband, forget your damn pride for one single minute and *focus*."

Barker stopped in the middle of the sidewalk. "I'm chasing because I'm lost, Jon. For the past twenty years, I've found people using breadcrumbs no bigger than a speck of dust. But this one, this case...until we find Rutherford or figure out who the girl is...I'm running on empty."

The regret in his voice was genuine, and for the first time ever, DJ felt sorry for the man. It was like watching his favorite quarterback make it to the Super Bowl and throw one bad pass after another.

After five years of looking up to Barker, it seemed weird to be the one on the consoling end of things, but DJ tried anyway. He said, "Then that's what we'll focus on. We haven't lost yet, Barker. We can't win them all, but our game, and Sara's game, they're not over yet."

Barker's cell phone rang. "Barker...uh-huh...she is? Right...okay, we'll be there in couple."

"Hospital?"

"Stardust is awake. She's ready to talk."

CHAPTER 14
SARA

Sara walked with her hands held out in front, trying to block the limbs from smacking her in the face.

On the slim chance that she could possibly identify him, she'd tried a more conversational approach, hoping to coax out more information. She asked questions about her husband and where the ring had come from. If he knew Brian and had he ever met him before. If he had any details about his disappearance. She asked what he liked to read, what the last movie was that he'd seen. What his favorite cereal was, what his *son's* favorite cereal was. Anything to spark a reaction, but she was ignored and had been given more yanks or tugs or shoves each time she'd asked a question. When he'd pushed too hard and she'd fallen, losing a layer of skin from both knees, she gave up and let him guide her.

They'd been hiking uphill and down, twisting left and right, and the sounds of exertion were evident in her captor's labored breathing.

The bastard's out of shape. If I knew where to go, I could run. Just play the game. You can't win that way.

She'd been without sight for so long that she could almost get a picture of their surroundings using her hearing. Somewhere deep in the woods. She could smell damp earth and pine trees. The stream's gurgling had faded a while back, so they were steadily moving away from it, farther into the forest, higher into whatever hill they might be climbing. The ground leveled out, and the surface changed underneath her feet, became softer and more malleable.

Is that grass? Pine needles? That's a new smell...what is that? Smells like a wet campfire.

The last time she'd been camping was on their fifth anniversary, the weekend the twins were conceived. Too much red wine had resulted in risqué sex out in the open, under the stars, and the next morning, she wasn't sure the fun had been worth the raging hangover. It'd rained in the middle of the night and the smell of the smoldering, soaked campfire had made her roiling stomach worse.

To test the echoes nearby, she raised her voice and asked, "Where are we?" The sound bounced off something big and solid in front of her.

Her guide said, "Cabin."

"Whose?"

"Nobody's."

"Does Nobody mind that you're using his cabin to hold a woman hostage?"

"Abandoned."

"Perfect. Abandoned cabin, middle of the woods. Mother of three with a desperate loser being controlled by a psychopath. I think I've seen this on Lifetime."

"Step."

"What?"

"Step."

Her foot caught on something and she tripped forward, realizing he meant *steps*. She lifted her leg, tested the area ahead, and placed her foot down. Pushed herself up, and felt for the next one. The wood sagged in the middle and creaked under her weight. "How many?"

"Three."

Up she went. With both feet safely on the porch, she said, "This might be easier if you said more than one word at a time."

"Unlikely."

She felt a hand on her back, pushing her forward. Heard the metallic screech of rusted hinges as a door swung open. She walked through and felt the cooler temperature inside on her skin. Smelled the musty scent of age and interior dampness of something that had been shuttered and neglected for far too long.

The door slammed shut.

He said, "Blindfold."

She took it off, relieved to have the use of her eyes again, but they hurt from the sudden rush of light pouring in through the cracked and broken windows. They cast their glow on an old wood stove squatting in the corner. She looked around the open room, saw a table with a single chair, an empty shelf. A decrepit bed with metal railings, a sagging mattress, and a sleeping bag. A red cooler, the kind used for picnics and long trips.

Is this my cage? I can do this. I can do this. Twenty-four hours.

"I'm staying here?" she asked, looking around and up at him. He towered over her, dressed all in black, the familiar ski mask taking place of the baseball cap and sunglasses. Ice blue eyes stared back at her.

"There," he said, pointing to a door in the back of the room.

"What's in there?"

"Cage."

"And what's all this stuff? Sleeping bag, cooler. You're staying here with me?"

"Observation."

"So this is it, huh?"

She angled her head upward, stepped closer to him. Aggressive, but contained.

Be strong, be strong, be strong.

She said, "If you are who I *think* you are, understand one thing, you big bastard. I've seen your face, and if things don't go well for me, this place will look like a five star resort compared to where you're going. I hope your son doesn't mind talking to his daddy behind a glass wall. Got me?"

His eyes narrowed. "Understood."

Control. For the first time in hours, control. At least a little bit. Enough to give her a renewed feeling of hope.

But what if he's lying, Sara? Trying to throw you off? This level is supposed to be about confusion, isn't it? He probably doesn't have a son. For God's sake, use your head. This isn't supposed to be easy.

Shut up. It's all you've got. Ask him something about Teddy. Scare him some more.

"Can I ask you one more question?" Sara thought she heard a muffled huff of exasperation through the ski mask.

"Another?"

"How much is he paying you?"

"He?"

"Teddy. Your boss, my shit-for-brains coworker. The guy who has my kids. How much is he paying you?"

His first response that contained more than a single word might as well have been a fist in the center of her chest.

"Not a *he*."

He pulled a black, cloth sack from his pocket and, as she tried to comprehend, shoved it over her head before she could stop him. He grabbed her by the neck, his large hand wrapping halfway around it as he forced her toward the back of the room.

Sara could hear the door opening, then he shoved her inside. The door slammed. He struck a match and a *whoosh* of flames followed. He removed the hood and she shielded her eyes from the light of a hissing gas lantern as they readjusted. A large dog cage sat in front of her, partially covered with a black blanket.

And sitting behind it, along one of the windowless walls, was an unconscious, bound and gagged man.

In the soft burn of the lantern, it wasn't difficult to make out the shirtless, miniature form of Teddy Rutherford.

***

Everything that Sara had anticipated, everything that she thought she knew, imploded like an old building brought to the ground with a bevy of well-placed explosives.

"*Teddy!*" she said. "What's he doing here?"

"Waiting," said the tall man.

"Waiting for what?"

"Pain," he said, motioning toward the table.

Beside the lantern were four objects she hadn't noticed before. A blowtorch, a knife, a set of clipping shears, and a cleaver.

If Teddy's here, then who has the kids? Who've I been talking to this whole time?

What if Teddy wants you to think he's being tortured?

Teddy slowly lifted his head. Sara watched him blink and then his eyes went wide as he focused on her. He mumbled a surprised, "Sara! Sara!" through the gag, then added something that sounded like, "Help me!"

Her notion that this was part of Teddy's plan disappeared as the tall man walked over, pivoted, and swung a bowling ball fist into his jaw. The crunch was sickening as Teddy's head whipped to the side and then flopped down to his chest, the blow knocking him unconscious.

"Why?" she said. She didn't know what to think, how to feel. Her emotions were bundled up with the promised confusion and tossed into the well of her consciousness. Switching to pity after so many hours of focusing her rage on Teddy was...difficult.

But she did.

As much as she detested him back in the real world, seeing his slumped, limp body straining against the ropes set her bottom lip to quivering. He was sleazy, offensive, and deceitful, but whatever sins he committed on the rest of humanity weren't deserving of this. Why was he here? What purpose did it serve to torture Teddy in front of her?

Confusion, Sara. Distraction. She wants you to know that you were wrong.

Who?! Who is SHE?!

Someone at the office. She knew I'd think it was him. He's the obvious choice.

The tall man said, "In," as he pointed toward the cage.

Sara looked down, saw the padlock on the cage's door. *Keys open locks, locks open cages. She wants me to cage myself. Why? What does that prove?*

Control. She can make you do whatever she wants.

"I'm not getting in that thing," she said.

"Expected." The tall man grabbed the blowtorch, ignited it, and shoved the flame at Teddy's bare shoulder. His skin seared and the sudden shock of pain brought him back to life.

His muffled scream clawed at Sara's eardrums. She dropped the paper bag, covered her ears, tried to block the sound of his wailing. "Enough!" she said. "I'll get in, I'll get in. No more, okay?"

Seconds later, she sat inside the cage, the door open in front of her, padlock dangling from it.

"Key," the tall man said.

She flung it at his legs.

He closed the cage door with a clank and a rattle, snapped the padlock shut with a click.

The black blanket covered half the cage, making it darker inside, blocking her view of Teddy. The metal rungs dug into her skin, pressing through her running shorts and into her thighs, her buttocks. She tested the distance of the sides, the top, each of them a half an arm's length away. It gave her room to move, to turn around if she needed.

Sara had never been claustrophobic, but the feeling of confinement overpowered her mind as it crawled its way over her body, sending her breathing into short, ragged bursts. Her chest hurt from straining to get enough oxygen. Fingertips tingled. Dizzy. The floor tilted underneath.

The tall man said, "Calm."

Teddy whimpered behind her, inhaling heavily through his draining nose, exhaling around the slobber-soaked rag.

Sara dumped the contents of the paper bag onto the cage's floor. The water bottle bounced. The apple rolled and settled. The jewelry box landed with a *thunk* and came to rest against her foot. She kicked it away, held the bag up to her mouth and breathed. Inhaling, exhaling, inflating the bag with air, sucking it back into her lungs.

Inhaling. Exhaling. Inhaling. Exhaling. Bringing herself to a controlled cadence.

Tempered normality returned. The tall man knelt down, shoved a familiar slip of paper through the bars.

"Instructions," he said.

She snatched it from his hand, held it around to read in the light.

SECOND HALF OF LEVEL 2 – SELF-
PRESERVATION
HIS PAIN = YOUR COMFORT
REMEMBER – 24 HOURS
IF YOU THINK HARD, THE ANSWER WILL COME.

His pain equals my comfort? God, this is insane. If I get hungry? Thirsty? If I have to pee? Torture Teddy, get rewarded.
She wants to see how selfish you are.

The tall man rattled the door. "Understood?" he asked, returning her earlier threat, returning to control.

"Yes," she said. "But she won't break me."

He nodded and slid another slip of paper through the cage.

This one read:

SO PREDICTABLE
HIS PAIN = YOUR CLUES
SOLVE THIS RIDDLE AND THE FIRST ONE IS
FREE
WHAT IS GREATER THAN GOD, MORE EVIL
THAN THE DEVIL?
THE POOR HAVE IT. THE RICH NEED IT. AND IF
YOU EAT IT, YOU WILL DIE.

Sara almost laughed with relief. Sometimes luck aligns with the universe.

Two weeks earlier, Lacey had come home from school with the exact same riddle and had flaunted it at her for hours. She had been tired and cranky after another day of dealing with Teddy's inadequacies and Jim's demands. She'd wanted to relax and unwind, to forget about the day, and Lacey's teasing had been so relentless that Sara had almost sent her to her room. The threat had worked well enough for her daughter to apologize and give her the answer.

Sara wadded up the slip of paper and threw it at the cage wall, toward the tall man's face. He didn't flinch. She said, "The answer is *nothing*."

"Quick." He slid yet another slip of paper into the cage.

CONGRATULATIONS. YOUR FIRST CLUE:
WHY DO I HAVE BRIAN'S WEDDING RING?
LITTLE ONE'S PAIN = MORE CLUES

LITTLE ONE'S PAIN = YOUR COMFORT
HOW MUCH DO YOU WANT TO KNOW?

Little One...she knows his nickname.

When she finished reading, she peered through the bars, glared at the tall man. "Are you done?"

"Temporarily," he said, sliding the black blanket over the cage, covering her in darkness, wrapping her in a shroud of solitary confinement. The only thing that penetrated her square tomb was the steady sound of Teddy's erratic, panicked breathing.

CHAPTER 15
DJ

DJ walked beside Barker down the hospital hallway, passing busy nurses and a couple of doctors who had their noses buried in clipboards. He had mixed feelings about the place. Spend enough time interviewing victims, you got to see every aspect of the darker side of humanity and what people are capable of doing to one another. But, on the opposite end of the spectrum, it also offered the prospect of seeing the power of human strength, resolve, and will. How hospitals managed to be simultaneously uplifting and demoralizing was as much of a mystery as the one they were trying to solve.

They located Room 323 and walked in, finding Anna lying in bed, a nurse hunched over her, checking her pulse. The nurse pushed her patient's hair back from her face, and told them to keep it short—doctor's orders. They agreed, then waited until she left to approach their only lead in a case that was falling apart faster than a house of cards.

Anna tried to smile, croaked out a raspy, "Hi," and then cringed when she tried to readjust herself upward.

DJ held up a hand, urging her back down. "No need to get up. Save your energy."

"Thanks," she said, voice dry and hoarse.

DJ looked at the swollen and bruised face. Lips puffy, eyes black. Long scrape down her cheek. He could see her former beauty underneath all the destruction. Felt his stomach fill up with pity and anger.

Barker said, "Getting along okay? Full recovery?"

"Something like that."

"Your husband knows you're here?"

"On his way. He didn't want Hank to see me like this, so he's dropping him off at my mom's house."

"Good idea," DJ said.

"Hank's a great name," Barker added. "Strong."

"My grandfather's name. So, I guess you want to know how I got—how I got so pretty, huh?"

DJ pulled a seat up beside the bed, sat down face to face with her. "Just a few questions, if you're up for it."

Barker leaned against the windowsill, crossed his arms. "Can you remember what happened?"

"She said her name was Deana."

Barker said to DJ, "D on the necklace?" then to Anna, "Did she give you a last name?"

"No. Didn't say much about herself. She asked me a lot of stuff, though."

"Personal questions?"

"Just stuff about stripping and if I liked it. Where I got my outfits, what my family thought. I didn't tell her I was married with a kid. Gotta keep the fantasy alive. I'm not bi, like some of the other dancers are, so I wasn't really into her, you know? But she kept flirting with me and I figured I'd play along, get some extra tips out of it. No harm in that, right? Money is money."

"Understandable. We spoke with Mildred, got a physical description. Anything stand out to you? Anything identifiable? Any chance you remember the necklace she was wearing?"

Dead end, Barker. Let it go. Just a necklace.

Anna shook her head. "Necklace? No, but she was attractive. About my age. Oh, she had one blue eye and one brown eye. Like that actress. I can't remember her name."

"Different colored eyes? You mean like two different colors of contacts?" Barker asked, scribbling something down on his notepad.

DJ said, "I think it's a disease."

"Let's check into that. Now, Mrs. Townsend, we were informed that you and some of the other girls offer, uh, offer...*after hours* dances. Is that true?"

Anna tried to roll over to face Barker, but the depth of her pain was evident. She winced and flopped onto her back. "If I say yes, will I get in trouble?"

"That hospital bed says you're free from judgment, the way I see it."

"Same here," DJ said. "It's important that we know the truth. This woman could be involved in another case we're investigating, and we need to know exactly what happened."

He watched the physical discomfort morph into mental anguish on her face. Eyes leaking tears. Her bottom lip, swollen and split-skinned, began to quiver. She inhaled deeply, tried to fight it.

"You have to understand—this whole thing—it's not easy for me. For us. My husband, he's been out of work for over a year. He and my son mean everything to me, and no matter how hard I try to keep my chin up and say, 'It pays the bills,' I hate it. Every second of it. But you wouldn't believe how much some of these pricks will pay to have you all to themselves."

A knock at the door interrupted them. The nurse poked her head in, reminded them to keep it short, and was gone as quickly as she had appeared.

"She's right," DJ said. "You need your rest, so let's fast forward a little bit. She offered you money for a private dance back at her home?"

"Ten *thousand* dollars, Detective."

Barker whistled.

"She showed me the roll of bills. Flipped through so that I could see it was really filled with hundreds. I couldn't say no."

DJ sat back. It was all a ruse, of course, but the amount was staggering, and it was easy to see how a young mother with an unemployed husband could get sucked in by the promises. "And then what happened? Mildred mentioned the woman left around two-thirty and you at three o'clock. Did you meet her somewhere?"

"Out in front of the club. She was waiting in her car."

"Any chance you remember what it was?"

"Some hybrid. Blue. Look, I want you to know that we're broke and desperate, and I realize how dangerous it is, but believe me, Detective, I'm usually *very* careful when I go somewhere for a private dance. I don't *ever* get into a car with someone and *always* follow them to their house."

"What was different this time?"

"The amount." She put a hand on her forehead. "Nobody had ever offered that much before. And she seemed nice enough...but don't they all? She insisted it would be okay. Over and over again. And I thought I'd lose the money if I didn't. Look where it got me. Look at my face. What was I thinking?"

Barker moved away from the window, walked over and took her hand in his. "Young lady," he said, "at my advanced age, I've learned some things, and one of them is this...beating yourself up won't do you any good. Don't make a bad situation worse."

"It's my fault," she said, wiping her eyes with her free hand.

"You were looking out for your family, and that's just as good of a reason as any. Blame the bastards that did this, not yourself. And I don't want to hear another peep out of you about it being your fault. Sound good to you?"

She nodded.

"That said, we need to hear what happened before they kick us out of here. You want a little payback, give us some details."

"It's so not like me, but I got into the car with her, we drove about a block, and then I felt a hand grab me from behind and somebody shove a rag over my mouth."

DJ said to Barker, "Chloroform."

"Yep."

"I tried to fight it, but I woke up half-naked in this basement. Ball gag shoved in my mouth. I could barely breathe. She was standing over me, smiling. Had a guy with her."

DJ thought, *Rutherford?* The silent look from Barker suggested he was thinking the same thing. DJ said, "Short guy? What did he look like?"

"No, super tall. Like, massive. Had a mask on."

Damn...but at least it confirms a third person. "Have you ever heard the name Teddy Rutherford?"

"No."

"Thought not. Sorry for interrupting. Then what happened?"

"She leaned over—and it's fuzzy—but I think she said something like, 'If you make a sound, you'll never see your family again.' I was so scared at that point, but I had no idea what was coming. This is the part I'll never forget. The rest is blurry, but I remember this exactly. She said, 'It's a shame we have to damage such a beautiful thing,' then she looks at the guy and goes, 'Don't leave her alive.' She left, and he started punching and punching and punching. His fists felt like cinderblocks. But I'm still here, so either he didn't listen, or he didn't hit me hard enough."

DJ shuddered. After years of working cases and seeing the worst of the human condition, making himself immune to such reactions remained impossible, and in truth, he hoped he never lost it, unlike Barker. The cantankerous veteran was able to let it slide off like rain on a slicker, and his display of sympathy with Anna was a rare one, but DJ used the emotional connection as a reminder that this was more than a paycheck.

Anna, as young as she was, had plenty of good decades in front of her, and she would have to live with that haunting memory for the rest of her life. He reached over, patted her arm. "Get some rest," he said. "You've been a big help."

"Hang on," Barker said. "How'd you get free?"

"That's the weird part. When I woke up, the ropes were untied."

"Huh. Interesting..."

DJ and Barker exited and walked down the hallway. Seconds later, a younger guy, clean-cut and in a hurry, rushed past them in the direction of her room.

Barker said, "Reckon that was the husband?"

"Yeah," DJ said. "Poor bastard's in for a shock, huh?"

"No doubt in my mind that girl ain't ever going back to stripping again. She's lucky to be alive."

They stepped into the elevator, waited on the door to close. DJ asked, "Why *is* she still alive? Why leave a witness? Why would he untie her?"

"Hell if I know. Guilty conscience? Dissention in the ranks?"

"Your guess is as good as mine. But we do need to check out the blue eye, brown eye thing."

"Haystack, needle. Needle, haystack."

"No more than Sara's husband and that damn necklace. It's all we've got to go on, Barker." The elevator chimed, signaling the ground floor. They stepped out, stopping in the hallway. DJ put his hands on his hips, defiant. "And who was it that suggested the idea that she might have been planted in Rutherford's basement?"

Barker snorted, said, "I suppose it would be the same dingleberry who's asking the question. Just because she woke up in his basement and Rutherford wasn't in the room doesn't mean he didn't know she was there. He could've been upstairs."

"It doesn't make any *sense*, Barker. If he's working with the necklace girl and the goon, collecting trophies or whatever, why not show up for the fun? What's the purpose?"

"Does it *have* to have a purpose? We're dealing with a couple of freaks, JonJon. We can profile all the hell we want, but if you try to read a psychopath's mind—"

"'*You'd have a better chance reading tea leaves in a blender.*' I know. I know."

"But, you're right, Captain Interruption, her screwed up eyes are the only solid thing we have to go on, so where do you suggest we start?"

DJ had been thinking about this from the moment Anna had mentioned it. He told Barker that they had to go with the closest connections. Sara and Teddy Rutherford both worked together at LightPulse. They had to consider the possibility that he had an accomplice there. It was a stretch, but they had to start narrowing down the possibilities somewhere. Medical records were protected by both Federal and State laws, and they didn't have enough solid evidence for a subpoena. "But," he said, "we can check photo IDs, look at criminal records. See if anybody pointed out mismatched eyes in their reports."

It'd be easy enough to take the list of employees and examine them across the board.

"Good idea," Barker admitted. "And if we come up with *nada*?"

"What're the chances that she'd use her own car to drive off with someone she planned to kidnap and murder? We check the rental companies for a blue hybrid. Narrow that list down to all the women that have rented one in the past few days."

Barker reached up, slapped DJ on the shoulder. Smiled.

"What?"

"I might've taught you a thing or two over the years, cowboy. You're wet behind the ears, but at least you're standing up for what you think is right. For once."

"Was that a compliment?"

"Don't let your head swell up. I don't have enough wisdom to fill it." Barker's cell rang. "Barker...yeah...at the hospital...What?...Where?...Okay, we're on it." He hung up, shook his head.

DJ raised an eyebrow.

Barker said, "Damn, I thought it couldn't get any stranger. They found Rutherford's car."

"And no Rutherford?"

"No Rutherford, but plenty of bloodstains."

CHAPTER 16
SARA

Sara tried to straighten her legs. The cage closed in; the metal bars formed the sides of a coffin. The absence of light was so complete that she could have been buried alive, under mounds and mountains of dirt, under roots and worms, under rocks and a thick gravestone. The only reminder that she was indeed alive was Teddy whimpering and shuffling behind her. Outside the cage, but inside his own prison. Inches and miles away.

Hours had passed. Or was it minutes? Time doesn't stand still in a vacuum, but in the absence of everything else, it loses all form, becomes elusive and teasing. Taunting with its childish game of 'catch me if you can'.

Sara shifted to one side, rubbed the skin on her behind, massaging out the deep crevices left by the thin, metal wiring. Toes numb. Back aching from being hunched over for so long. Neck stiff and throbbing. She could smell the dried sweat on her running clothes. Felt guilty for wanting the luxury of a shower when the world around her was covered in physical and emotional blackness.

Sara pawed the cage floor and found the bottle of water. Took a small sip, rationing what remained. Partly as preservation, partly as a preventative. The tingling sensation in her bladder wasn't going away, no matter how hard she tried to direct her thoughts elsewhere. She refused to allow her abductor the satisfaction of torturing Teddy to get what she wanted. She would piss on the floor inside her cage before she would give in.

I won't let them win, she thought. *I won't.*

Sara twisted Brian's ring around her thumb, feeling the sweat between skin and metal.

Why...why...his wedding ring...his ring...his ring...oh my God... she knows what happened to him...she knows...

How? Unless she kidnapped him, too? Stole him from me. Took him away.

She knows...she knows...maybe he...maybe he was having—

No. No, no, no, don't think like that. He wouldn't.

Would he? An affair?

Not Brian. He wouldn't...there were never any signs...I never suspected anything...

You know that's not true...

...the receipt...

Teddy moaned behind her, followed by the dull scrape of wood on wood as the chair legs scratched against the floor. Then, silence. Nothing more. Back to the darkened depths of her solitude.

She took a small sip of water, just enough to wet her tongue.

Brian...what did you do?

The receipt, the one that had fallen out of the book he'd been reading on his trip to San Diego. Two meals at a restaurant. A bottle of wine.

Brian never drank wine...hated it. Hated the taste. It made him sick.

At the time, she hadn't questioned it. Business trip. Colleagues with a taste for expensive Bordeaux. Trying to woo a new client at a conference. It meant nothing. Less than nothing. An innocuous drink with someone who had money to invest. Choked it down with a smile to earn a hefty commission.

But was that it? Was that all?

She thought back to all the connections she'd made earlier in the day, back when she'd thought it might've been a woman, back when she thought it might've been someone inside LightPulse. The mention of a breakaway, the mini-bomb idea that led her to believe it was Teddy.

A woman at the office...was Brian having an affair with one of the girls at work?

No, couldn't be. He was in San Diego.

They could've met him there. Was anyone on vacation then? Anyone missing from the office?

I can't remember...so long ago...

Sara's stomach churned. The realization of a deeper truth to his disappearance took her breath away, tightened its grip around her lungs. Made her head swim, made her dizzy. She rubbed her eyes, wiped a tear from her cheek.

What did I do, Brian? Was it me? Did you not love me anymore?

The betrayal. The anguish. The pain. It was too much. All those years of loving a man who would dare to take another woman to bed. Had it been going on for some time? Or was it a single act of indiscretion? Too much wine? Promises to do all the things between the covers that they had grown too tired and bored and busy to do? Their relationship had *seemed* great. To her. To her family. To everyone who complimented them. To her friends, who admitted to jealousy over the emotional connection they had.

It was true that their sex life had faded to once or twice

a month. Brief encounters when they had enough energy to squeeze it in after long days, after the kids had gone to bed. It was the typical scenario of many busy marriages, something they'd discussed and were excited to fix, but he'd gone missing before they'd had the chance.

Went missing, or left intentionally for another woman?

She wanted to run away, leave, disappear. Evaporate into a fine mist and escape the cage walls. But, she was trapped, contained, forced to deal with her regret and sorrow with no way out.

Sara drew her knees up to her chest, buried her face in her arms.

Damn you, Brian. Who was it? Who was she?

Someone at the office...which one? Who was there two years ago when he disappeared? Me. Susan. She wouldn't...Kara and Sandra in R&D. Mandy at the front desk. She was cute. Her? Jenny in Accounting. Not his type. What was the office manager's name, the one who retired...Janet...Janet? Too old.

Six of them. All gone. All moved on to different places in their lives. New jobs, higher paying jobs. Motherhood. From what she'd heard, they were all living in Portland, except for Janet, who'd moved to Key West.

This woman knows about stuff in the new Juggernaut...all the women who used to be there are gone, so if he was cheating...she's been hired since he disappeared...

Why do that? Why get so close to me if she was sleeping with my husband?

Keep tabs on me? Make sure I wasn't getting closer to finding him?

Such a stretch. Somebody could be breaking the NDA, passing along info.

Lots of new faces...Shelley and Amy and Wendy and Shay and Christina...

Was it possible? Could any of the women who were there now be the one who had destroyed her life? Damaged her children's lives? Still so many questions, still no closer to a reasonable answer. The possibilities were endless. So were the motivation and reasoning. It didn't make any sense. None of it.

And what if she was completely off? What if Brian hadn't been having an affair, and the woman was some psycho targeting her family for some unknown reason? She had access to confidential LightPulse information, but it didn't mean she was actually *inside* the company. And it could be one of the men, a partner, passing along details. What if they had murdered Brian, taken his ring, kept it all this time in order to torture her, toy with her, make her play a game? Was it a game of life and death? Was that really what was going on?

I need to know more. Teddy...his pain...more clues...

No, don't. You can figure this out.

How? I know nothing. One...two...three...seven...eight. Eight other women in the office. It could be any one of them. And if it's one of the guys...how many women do they know? It's impossible. Why does she have Brian's wedding ring? No idea. None whatsoever. Affair? Maybe. Kidnapped him and took it? Murdered him and took it? Why me? Why now? Why two years later?

I could ask Teddy...what if he saw her face?

She clambered around inside the cage, felt the metal bars digging into her knees. She thought about tugging at the blanket, slipping it off so she could see him, but that would be against the rules. Breaking them would result in another phone call, another scream from one of her children in pain because she refused to obey.

"Teddy," she whispered. *"Teddy.* Wake up."

Sara cocked an ear, listened over her shoulder. Tried to hear any movement coming from the other room. Earlier, who knows how long ago, she'd heard the tall man moving around, followed by the front door slamming. Was he gone? Sitting on the front porch? Taking a leak out in the woods?

I need to pee...almost hurts...

"Teddy? Can you hear me?"

She heard him inhale, imagined him waking up, opening his eyes. Panic setting in as he realized that it wasn't a dream, that he was tied to a chair in a pitch black room. He mumbled her name through the gag. It came out as a question, testing the space in front of him, like he was unsure if her voice was truly there.

"I'm here, Teddy, I'm here. Keep your voice down, okay?"

His response was muffled and wet. "Okay."

"Are you in pain?"

"A lot."

"I'm sorry. Listen to me. Listen. Everything will be okay. We'll get out of here. I'll get you out, I promise."

"What's...what's going on?"

She could tell it was difficult for him to speak, difficult to push his words around the cloth binding his mouth open. "Someone's playing a game with me."

"A game?"

"A bad one. They have my kids."

"What?"

"They've been kidnapped." She scooted close to the cage wall, wrapped her fingers through the bars and whispered, "How'd you get here? Did he bring you?"

"The guy...him."

"Not so loud, okay? He's working with some woman, any idea who?"

"No. A voice...on a phone."

"What did she say?"

"Said I...said I deserved this. For being...a pig."

"I think it's somebody at the office."

"Said I'm...motivation."

"Motivation? Teddy, focus. Who's doing this?"

"Don't know."

"Anything at all. Think. Guess."

"Don't know."

"Teddy, please. Say the first name that comes to your mind."

The seconds ticked by. He was silent for so long, Sara thought he might've passed out again. Finally, he mumbled, "Maybe—maybe it's—"

The door crashed open, slamming against the wall hard enough for Sara to feel the vibrations through the floor. Thundering footsteps, followed by, "Quiet!" The voice echoed off the walls as Sara screamed, pushing herself up against the far side of the cage, away from him. Light from the open door penetrated the black cloth enough to illuminate the interior. She could see her hands shaking.

The sickening *thuds* of fists on flesh replaced the noise of her gasping. It sounded like someone with a sledgehammer beating a dead animal carcass.

Teddy coughed and gagged. Moaned. She was almost

relieved that she couldn't see what was happening to him, but the images in her mind were just as bad.

One, two, three more punches, and then it stopped.

The black cloth whipped open and the tall man knelt down in front of her.

"Don't hurt him again," she begged.

"Penalty," he said, slipping another note through the cage.

Sara grabbed it. Hands unsteady, paper flapping like a wounded dove. She didn't want to read it, terrified of what it might contain. What penalty had she brought upon herself? What had she done by breaking a rule? If it was for her, she'd take it. She would take the punishment.

Not the kids...not the kids...don't hurt them anymore...I'll play...I'll play...

Fingers trembling and uncooperative, she fumbled the note open.

THE PENALTY IS SEVERE. NO MORE CLUES. NO QUESTION FOR THIS ROUND.
AND NOW YOU MUST CHOOSE YOUR PATH:
1. HE DIES – YOUR CHILDREN ARE SAFE AND YOUR CAGE TIME ENDS
2. HE LIVES – I'LL REVEAL WHO I AM BUT THERE MAY BE CONSEQUENCES

One simple choice that changed the game completely. Sara dropped the note to the cage floor. It was easy. The first option was clear: order Teddy's death and the kids would be fine. The ambiguity of the second choice left her wondering. It didn't say anything about harming Lacey,

Callie, and Jacob, just that she would reveal her identity.

She won't do anything to hurt them. The game is over if she does. I can't risk it. I can't. It's not—it's not even a choice.

She'd read about questions like these before. Psychological tests designed to assess compassion. A passenger train is speeding down the tracks, a single person in its path. Derail the train to save one man and risk countless lives, or run him over and save everyone on board? The problem with the question was the lack of guarantee that anyone would die in the first option.

But this...this was different. There were no alternatives.

She would have to play God. Choose when and where someone died. The remainder of her days would be spent wondering what might've happened if she had picked the second option, but the regret would pale in comparison to what she'd feel if she had read too far into it and something happened to her babies.

The tall man said, "Choose."

"Give me a minute."

She listened to Teddy's breathing.

He was clueless. His fate contained in a simple slip of paper. No idea that he was about to die. *Had* to die. If he knew what the note said, would he offer himself as a sacrifice? Would he say, 'Do it, save them,' or would he be the same self-centered, egotistical brat that he'd always been? Could he, for once, let go of his self-absorption and care about another person? She'd heard stories of soldiers jumping on hand grenades, surrendering their lives to save others. That level of personal disregard was almost incomprehensible. She would do it for the children. Would Teddy? If he knew what was at stake, would he make that choice?

He wouldn't. He would come up with an excuse. Run if he could.

Forcing away her pity didn't make the decision any easier. But, she only had one to make.

She kicked the cage, close to the tall man's face, surprising him. Watched him fall backwards, landing on his ass. "Number one," she said.

He grunted, groaned, crawled back to his feet. Grabbed the cage and shook it. His only form of retaliation.

Sara thought about kicking his fingers, smashing them against the bars.

He pulled a handgun from his waistband, screwed a silencer into the barrel. Pointed it at her head.

She lifted her arms, knowing the fleshy shield would do no good, but it was a natural reaction.

"Watch," he said, throwing the blanket off the cage, revealing the room.

Teddy was a crumpled mass, bloodier and covered with extra bruises. His body purple and limp. Unconscious, unaware of his impending death.

The tall man lifted his gun, pointed, and paused.

Paused.

Paused.

Paused.

Sara screamed, "Don't—" as he pulled the trigger.

CHAPTER 17
DJ

DJ sat at his desk, going over a list of LightPulse's female employees while Barker went to check out Rutherford's car for any evidence. The initial feedback had been discouraging, but the Bloodhound was on a trail, and there was no convincing him otherwise.

There were nine women at LightPulse, including Sara, and he'd turned up nothing significant on the first five. Mostly clean, a traffic ticket or two, one instance of a Minor in Possession. Young women fresh out of college. Still in party-mode, first real job, first real paycheck. None of them fit the profile of what he was looking for, but then again, did a sociopath ever reveal her true nature? And since Oregon didn't list eye color on driver's licenses, he examined their ID photos, enhancing them for clarity as much as possible, trying to discern different-colored irises. Considering any one of them could've been wearing contacts to hide that fact, he could almost hear Barker over his shoulder, telling him how pointless it was. Yammering on with some proverb that he'd heard hundreds of times over the years.

What I need, he thought, *is an outlier. Something that stands out.*

The next two proved to be as unrewarding as the rest. Grandmothers in their sixties. He didn't bother going through their information. It was unlikely either of them could be misconstrued as an attractive twenty-something with a possible boob job like the Ladyfingers bartender had suggested.

The last employee didn't come up in his Oregon DMV search. He checked the spelling of her name again. *Hmm...still driving with an out of state license, are we? How long have you been here? A couple of months...where are you from...where are you from...California.*

There you are, Shelley. Shelley Ann Sergeant. Formerly of San Diego...registered a tan SUV...California driver's license says your eyes are...green.

"Shit." DJ hurled his mouse at the nearby wall, the cheap plastic shattering into a dozen pieces. Heads whipped around, examined him, and then went back to their calls and case files. Amongst the cluttered desks, with keyboards clacking and phones ringing, frustrated outbursts were common enough that nobody paid much attention. As long as you didn't hurt anyone in the process, you got it out, you moved on. Standard norm for a group of people chasing wisps of information, trying to put jigsaw puzzles together in the dark.

Regardless, it'd been a long time since he'd had an outburst like that, and the embarrassment of losing his composure left his cheeks flushed. He crawled across the floor, scooped up the remnants and tossed them in the trashcan. Put his back against the wall.

We screwed up. Chased too many shitty leads. I'm wrong, Barker's been wrong about everything.

Sergeant Davis ambled up to DJ's desk, tossed a file down. "Judge denied your request, JonJon, not enough circumstantial to search the car rentals. Better luck next time, huh?"

DJ stared at the ceiling and beat the back of his head against the wall as Davis waddled away.

He called Barker, hoping he'd made some progress.

"Go for Barker."

"Any luck?"

"Waitress across the street saw a tall guy park the car sometime this morning. Said he left and never came back."

"Tall guy, huh? Think it's the same one?"

"Has to be. Too convenient."

"Can she identify him?"

"Dressed in black, dark hair. That's about it. Sent some blood samples back. Hope we'll be able to identify Rutherford from it, but we've got another clog in the drainpipes."

"What's that?"

"Found two receipts from yesterday in the center console. Guess where the first one's from?"

"Where?"

"No, really. Guess."

"Barker."

"Ladyfingers, for eighty-four dollars."

"Damn it. I was sure he—"

"Hold up now, don't get your panties in a wad. Time-stamped at eight-fifteen, so he was there, but considering the amount of blood in his car and the second receipt, I'm about to give in and say you were right."

"About what?"

"About Rutherford not being involved with Miss Stardust. Not directly, anyway. Ladyfingers is a connection, but the second one is from Hotel Llewellyn. Our boy may not have been home last night."

"Easier to frame somebody when they're not home."

"Doesn't mean he wasn't removing himself from the situation."

"If the connection's there, it's there, but I won't say I told you so about him not being involved."

"Wild ass guesses don't make you a genius, cowboy, but your instincts are getting better."

"Wouldn't worry about me being a genius. Came up empty on the heterochromia."

"The what?"

"The different colored eyes thing. None of the women at LightPulse have it, from what I can tell."

"Hate to break it to you, but I didn't figure she'd be that close to home. Where are you with the rental records?"

"Denied. Not enough evidence."

"No shit? I figured Carson would be all over this one. He's usually Quick Draw McGraw when it comes to missing kids."

"Guess it takes more than a stripper in a hospital bed. So, what's next?"

"Face time, JonJon. Ask questions. No more chasing ghosts. Gotta pound the ground before this one gets too far away from us."

"Like it hasn't already."

"Finish this one for me. When one door closes..."

"Another one opens?"

"No. You kick that son of a bitch off its hinges. Now get your chin off your chest, put your helmet on, and get back out there for the second half, got me?"

"Got it, coach."

"Back to the basics, DJ. I'm sticking with the car and the giant for now. Check for witnesses around the schools, check the babysitter—hell, check garbage cans. Check out anybody who's tweaked your whodunit instinct. We're missing something simple, I can feel it."

"Will do." DJ hung up, thinking, *If it were simple, Barker, we'd have figured it out already.*

***

DJ took out a notepad and began to draw a mind map of everything he knew about the case. Sara Winthrop and her three missing children were at the center of it all. The outward lines connected to Teddy Rutherford, Jim Rutherford, her assistant, Shelley, and the seven other women who worked at LightPulse. Willow Bluesong, the babysitter who hadn't been home when they'd stopped by. Reluctantly, he added Brian Winthrop, but only because he knew Barker would've demanded that he be included. He added the schools, their principles, the ice cream shop. The tall man, the mystery woman. Ladyfingers and Stardust. By the time he was finished, it looked like a never-before-seen constellation and sparked no new sense of direction.

He came up with a reason to draw an *X* over each person and place on the chart. Jim Rutherford had behaved oddly because he was trying to protect his son. Teddy Rutherford was either missing or dead. They knew almost nothing about the tall man or the mystery woman, except that they were working together. The schools had already told them everything they knew. He wrote 'Ghost' underneath Brian Winthrop's name and 'Collateral' under

Anna Townsend's.

He crossed out everyone with good reason.

Everyone except Willow Bluesong and Shelley Sergeant.

He decided to start with them, and if neither one could provide anything fresh, he'd move on to friends and family. Beyond that—as much as he hated the idea, and Barker loathed it because it made him feel inadequate—they would have to get the press involved.

The last they'd heard of Sara Winthrop, she was on foot, running away from the Rose Gardens. If she were still playing this game—

Are you ready to play the game?

—and if she were still racing around Portland, surely someone would've spotted a distraught and harried woman. They'd have to get pictures of her and her kids on the news, issue an alert.

It felt good to be going in a concrete direction, regardless of the fact that he had no idea where it was heading. The case hadn't gotten away from them yet, not completely, and he left for Willow Bluesong's house, excited that something tangible might be on the horizon.

She wasn't what he had expected.

"Mrs. Bluesong?" he asked when she answered the door.

"Yes?" she said, pushing her waist-length, graying braids over her shoulder. "Miss, actually," she added, smoothing down her tie-dyed dress.

The hesitant smile and ratty Birkenstocks screamed innocence, and DJ had to remind himself not to assume. *Ass out of you and me.* "Detective Johnson, ma'am."

She smiled. "And I'm Miss Willow, *sir.*"

"Mind if I ask you a few questions?"

"What's this about?"

"Sara Winthrop."

Her smile disappeared, her hand rushing up to cover her gaping mouth. "Is she okay?"

"May I come in?"

"She's not dead, is she?"

"Not that we—we're trying to—I think it's best that we sit down."

"How'd it happen?" She fell against the doorjamb.

"I'm sorry—I didn't mean—she's not dead...that we know of. Missing. She and her children."

"That you *know of?* What does that mean?"

He sighed. It never got any easier. A couple of wrong words and the message drifted like a rudderless boat. "We're assessing the facts. If you could give me five or ten minutes, I could use your help."

"But is she okay?"

"I—we don't know yet. But whatever you can offer—"

"I just saw her this morning. Oh God, okay. Come in, come in." She pushed the door open further and motioned him inside.

DJ stepped across the threshold, greeted by incense blended with the scent of freshly baked chocolate chip cookies. He followed her down the hallway, shoes squeaking on the hardwood floor. Dusty picture frames sat on dustier shelves. Miss Willow in her younger days, smiling beside a thin, scraggly man with a hippie mane and a ZZ Top beard. No children, except for the couple of recent photos where she posed beside Sara's kids, all of their smiles beaming. At a park, one perched above the other on a slide. Another with her balancing opposite them on a seesaw.

She led him into the living room, offered him tea and cookies as he sat on the brown, forest-print couch. He declined. She insisted.

And a couple of minutes later, DJ bit into one of the best chocolate chip cookies he'd ever tasted.

Miss Willow sat on the edge of her recliner, sipping her tea. "How—how serious is this, Detective?"

DJ sat the plate of cookies down on the coffee table, licked his fingers. "Unfortunately, we're treating it as a multiple kidnapping and a missing person, at least for now."

"Kidnapping? What happened?"

"Like I said, we're assessing the situation. As of right now, all four of them are missing. Under—we think under different circumstances."

"That's horrible."

"You said you saw Mrs. Winthrop and her children this morning?"

"She stopped by before she took them to school."

"And she sounded okay to you? Mention anything bothering her?"

She shook her head, blew cool air over the tea. "She was rushed. Who isn't with three kids? Don't get me wrong, I love the three of them like they're my own, but they're a handful."

"She was rushed?"

"Late for a meeting. Said something about Teddy, this coworker she doesn't like. That's not out of the ordinary.

And...what else...we talked about plans for this evening."

"Plans?"

"She was supposed to drop the kids off and then meet with another reporter. She's so busy these days. Magazines calling all the time. She manages it well, but I can tell it's getting to her."

"She's in magazines? What kind?" *Public spotlight, somebody's jealous?*

"Oh, those business ones. I can't keep up anymore."

"So she's successful?"

"Overnight, more or less. Within the past six months."

"Interesting. Crossed paths with anyone in that timeframe?"

Miss Willow sat her mug down on the table. "I know what you're getting at, Detective, but no, not that I know of. She can be—how do I say this—she can be a bit bullheaded at times. In my mind, though, it's all a part of the game."

Whoa...the game...are you ready to play the game? Did she slip up? No, not her. Can't be involved. What would Barker say? Something about fish and worms, probably.

DJ took a chance. Dangled the bait to see how she would react. He said, "Are you ready to play the game?"

She squinted at him, shook her head. "Pardon?"

Clueless. "Sorry, you reminded me of something my partner says. He rambles a lot."

"Oh."

"What do you mean by part of the game?"

"Nothing, really, just a figure of speech. She's mentioned stepping on some toes before, that's all. From what I remember, it wasn't anything that called for...oh, what's the word I'm looking for?"

"Retaliation?"

"Retaliation, that's it. She's a good woman, Detective Johnson. If she's—if she's okay, I can't imagine what she's going through. First her husband, and now this? What's the world coming to?" Miss Willow stared out the window. "When my husband passed, I didn't leave the house for months. But Sara's strong. Smart, too. So smart. I've never had any doubts about her."

"Right." DJ tapped his pen on the notepad. As pleasant as the woman was, he was wasting time. She was no more involved with the situation than any of the other worthless dead ends. "Couple more questions and I'll be on my way."

She kept her eyes locked on the world outside. "It would seem I'm free for the evening. Stay as long as you'd like."

"You mentioned her husband. How'd you feel about him?" He didn't want to ask any more pointless questions, but he knew that Barker would send him back if he failed to ask everything.

"Never met him. Sara and I didn't meet until after he was gone. The way she talked about him, the man was a saint."

"I'm sure it was hard on her."

"Not was. *Is.*"

"Definitely. Definitely." DJ took one last look at his notepad to see if he'd missed anything, reading over his mind map scribbles. *Nothing there...nothing there...she wouldn't know about Ladyfingers...let's see...* "Shelley Sergeant," he said. "Familiar with her?"

Miss Willow whipped her head around. "*That* girl?"

The vehemence in her voice made DJ sit up straighter. "What's—"

"Have you ever met someone who makes your skin crawl so much, you don't want to be in the same room with them?"

"All the time." For him, the sensation was another day at the office.

She said, "Wolf in sheep's clothing."

"What makes you say that?"

"I won't let her in my house anymore. Bad energy. Acts like a mouse to your face, but you watch her when she thinks nobody's looking. She wears this diamond necklace with the letters 'S.D.' I couldn't tell you what they really stand for, but in my mind, it might as well be *She-Devil.*"

DJ's notepad fell to the floor. *The necklace...*

CHAPTER 18
SARA

Sara pulled her hands away from her ears. The screams she heard weren't her own. Muted and muffled, they were coming from somewhere else within the room.

She glanced up, saw the tall man pointing the gun at Teddy. Silent. Motionless.

Flicked her head around.

Teddy's eyes bulged. He strained against his ropes, wailing through the fabric stretched across his mouth. He was alive. No fresh wounds. No bullet holes that she could see. A wet patch darkened the center of his khakis.

Sara reached down, felt the dryness of her running shorts. Somehow, she'd maintained control of her own bladder.

The tall man let the gun drop to his side, flopped down on the floor next to Sara's cage, and removed his ski mask. His dark, disheveled hair was twisted and tangled with a number of sprigs standing at attention.

Him. I can't believe I was right.

He shook his head, saying, "I couldn't...I couldn't do it."

Teddy's howls subsided to whimpers of relief.

Sara scooted to the cage wall, rested her forehead against the cool metal, staring at him. *What now? If he doesn't...the kids...* "Look at me," she said. "If you don't— my children—what'll happen to them?"

The same face, the one from the grocery store,

contorted with regret. The corners of his mouth curving downward. Eyes wide, uncertain. "I—I don't know."

"Can you lie? Can you tell her you did it?"

"She'll know. She always knows. Always, always."

"What's your name?"

"I can't—"

"What's your *name*?"

He slapped the gun barrel against his palm, looked out the door, then back to Sara. Wavered. "Michael."

"Michael, okay. I didn't want you to, I didn't, but my kids—what'll happen if you don't?"

"She'll come up with something."

"She who?"

"It was supposed to be simple."

"You mean the game?"

"I never thought I—God, how could I let myself—I always said no kids. No kids, ever." He growled in frustration, then slung the handgun upward and fired three shots into the ceiling.

The soft, dull *pop*s filled the room as Sara recoiled. She felt no pity for him, but sensed an opening. "Help me," she said. "Help me before she does something."

"She won't."

"How do you know?"

"Because they're not the endgame—you are."

Damn you, give me some clear answers. "Please," she said, "tell me what's going on."

"You should've figured it out by now."

Sara slapped the cage, felt the stinging in her palm. "Who *are* you people? If you're not going to help, at least let me out. I promise you, with every ounce of truth I have in me, that if you let me out of here, I won't say a word."

"I'm not stupid, Sara, if I let you—"

"Teddy won't, either, will you?"

Teddy looked up at the sound of his name, shook his head. "Nothing," he mumbled through the rag. "Never saw you."

"Not that easy," Michael said.

"It is," Sara said. "I promise. You'll never see us again. Let me out. Please, let me out."

"You don't know my sister, don't know what she's like. Your husband didn't, either. At least, not until he tried to leave her."

Sara's chest tightened. The inside of the cage felt smaller.

Oh, God...Brian...you didn't—you were...so it's true. I can't believe it.

"He was clueless. Tried to leave. He wanted to go home, wanted to get away. See if he could patch things up, you know?"

"Was that what she meant when she said I'd taken something from her? Because he wanted to come home?"

The crack in his dam widened. "More or less. Brian tried. The guilt ate at him all the time. He'd come to me, ask me what he should do, but what was I supposed to tell him? What he was doing was wrong, I absolutely know that, and I'm sorry for what you've had to go through, but how're you supposed to tell somebody that there *is no* escape? You can't look a guy in the face and say, 'If you leave, you're dead.' He wouldn't have believed me. Oh no, not my sweet, innocent little sister. She's too cute, too shy. Nobody knows what she's capable of. Nobody. There's something black inside her, something dark, and I can't do it anymore. No matter what I do for her, no matter how far I go to protect her or help her, there's no way to make up for the things that made her this way. I'm done, I'm done, I'm done."

What Sara wanted to say was, *Don't give me your bullshit sob story. I don't care what happened to either of you, and both of you can burn, for all I care.* But she was afraid he would leave her locked up, and she and Teddy would begin the slow, agonizing wait, biding their time in the godforsaken cabin until Death knocked at the door. And, as Sara listened to him talk, she struggled with the realization that a revelation was coming. One that she didn't want to hear, but had no ability to prevent herself from asking.

"Did you—did you kill him, Michael?"

Michael hung his head. "It was her. I just do the before and after. Wasn't ever able to cross that line like she can. But your husband, he definitely had some heart. I don't know how he lasted as long as he did. Too long. I couldn't watch anymore."

Sara fell back against the cage, removed Brian's ring from her thumb, twisted it between her fingers. Let it drop to the cage floor. It bounced, rattled about, and disappeared through the bars.

The tears wouldn't come.

There was hurt. There was an aching buried further down than whatever shallow grave contained Brian's body, but the brief respite of having some closure was enough to contain the sorrow. Mourning would come later, if she ever had another minute to herself, if she made it through this alive, if the day ever came when she would have the chance to look back and grieve. And if she were to have that opportunity, she had to play smart. Win him over.

She watched him scoot around, lean his head against the wall. He closed his eyes. Sara waved a hand at Teddy, catching his attention. She mouthed, "It'll be okay."

Teddy blinked twice.

I almost got him killed. How will I ever look at him again without thinking about that?

You won't. You owe him.

I wonder if he knows I had to choose...

Maybe, but will he care if you get him out of here?

If I explain what the note said...

Later. You still have to get out of this.

"Michael?"

"Yes?"

"What happened to your sister?"

"Long story."

"Well, you have a captive audience."

"How do you still have a sense of humor?"

"It's the only thing I have left."

"Good point."

"Your sister?"

"I know what you're doing."

"I'm curious."

"And a terrible liar."

"Was she abused?"

"You could say that."

"What would *you* say?"

"I wouldn't say anything. The past is the past." He climbed to his knees, lit the lantern, and sat back down.

The new light in the room revealed the extent of

Teddy's bruising, the snot draining from his nostrils. The wet patch between his legs had expanded to cover his crotch and the inside of his thighs.

Sara gawked at Teddy.

Michael said, "He can take a punch."

"Do you like hurting people?"

"Enough with the therapy session, Sara."

"I'm trying to understand."

"You wouldn't. You wouldn't. The things I had to watch them do to her..."

"Who, Michael? Who did those things?"

"You really want to know what happened? You really want to know why you're in a cage?"

"I can—"

"You can't *anything*, Sara. There's no helping her. Believe me, I've tried."

"What happened?"

Michael stood up, walked into the main room. She heard him rummaging around in the cooler, heard the sounds of ice clattering about. He came back with a beer, twisted off the cap, and drained the bottle. Pivoted, and hurled it out the door. The glass shattered. He said, "She—she has issues."

"Who doesn't?"

"Not like this. Not most people. Our dad—he left when we were kids. We never knew why. No reason. One day he stood up from the dinner table and walked out the door. Never saw him again. I didn't mind so much. He was strict. Mean. Drunk all the time, but my sister loved him like nothing else in the world. So when he left, it ruined her. Abandonment issues. Doesn't like people leaving her. That's why she does what she does when they try to leave. Melodrama, right? Like some bad TV show, like you said. But then Mom...she took a bunch of pills about a week later. We wound up in this foster home— God, I shouldn't be telling you this. She wouldn't like it."

"If you need to talk, talk. She'll never know."

Michael paced back and forth. "They made us call them Mother and Father. She *hated* them, hated, hated, hated, and they knew it, too. Our dad was a cupcake compared to them. And you want to know what made it worse? They adored me. I don't know why, maybe because I listened. Obeyed. They gave me anything I asked for, and Mother—Mother put her in a cage whenever she misbehaved. An actual cage, Sara.

"Locked her in a cage in a windowless bedroom, and she'd make her play these sadistic games to get out. I know it damaged her at first, but after a while—when she got older—I think she *enjoyed* it, and I swear she'd get thrown in there on purpose. I wish that I'd been able to do something sooner. Father didn't do a damn thing, and I couldn't do a damn thing to help her because I was too scared. I was eight years old—what could I do? But you— your husband—he tried to leave, and now she's taking it out on you. You see? You wanted to know, you wanted to know. See how it all fits together now? Do you? Huh? *Do you?* The game, the cage, torturing a mother? It was bad before, but this, it's too much. I'm done. No more."

Too far, too far, too far, Sara. Bring him back.

"Let's talk about something else, something better. Do you really have a little boy?"

"You got what you wanted to hear."

"I'm serious. I want to know, really. You've got a son?"

"Had."

"Had? What happened?"

"He's gone."

"Did your sister—"

"God, no," he interrupted. "He's with his mother."

"Do you see him much?"

"Never."

"Why?"

"She gave me a choice. No sister or no wife. When I told her I *had* no choice, she left. Haven't seen her or William since."

"Where are they?"

"No clue."

"Haven't you ever tried to find them?"

"That wouldn't be a good idea. She wouldn't like it."

"Your wife or your sister?"

"Sister."

"She has that much control over you?"

"I owe it to her."

"No you don't. You said so yourself, you're done. Take your life back."

"It's not that easy."

"It *can* be. You have my permission."

"I don't need your permission, Sara. What I need is for that little black cloud to be gone."

"She owns you."

"Owns? I guess that's the right word." He went quiet. The whispering lantern drowned out everything else in the room until he spoke again. "I think of her as another organ. Something inside me that a doctor's never seen before, like this thing that only lets my heart beat when she's ready to allow it."

"What if she's your appendix?"

"My appendix?"

"Something you could live without."

"It doesn't work that way."

"But what if it did?" Sara tried to stretch. Every muscle was cramping and aching again. "What if you could disappear?"

"She found me in Chicago. She found me in Atlanta. She found me in San Diego. I don't know how, but she always does. She finds me, draws me in again, and I have no control over it. She said if I tried to hide from her one more time...game over." He leaned against the wall, slid down to the floor.

The resignation in his voice, the defeated tone of it, gave Sara new hope. He'd tried and failed on his own, but if he had help, if he really wanted out... She said, "It might be game over for you, but not for me. Let me out, let me fight back. I'll fight with you, or even *for* you. You can be free. If you won't try, at least let me. Give me a chance."

"I can't. She'll never forgive me."

"Please, Michael. I want my kids to have a good life."

He said, "I wanted a good life. She wanted a good life."

"I know you did. We all do, but there's nothing I can do to change that. My kids still have a chance."

He rubbed a shaky hand across his face. Slapped the gun barrel against his palm again. *Slap...slap...slap*, like a ticking clock. "You'll have to get past Samson first."

"Samson?"

"One of her other slaves. The one who took your son this morning."

"*Other* slaves? How many more are there?"

"A couple. You had a tail while you were running."

"The girl on the bike, on the bridge."

"Her, yeah. Out of the picture, though. Samson, he's your biggest problem now."

"I'll figure it out. I can do it. You have to let me try."

"You won't win."

"You can't win if you don't play. Give me a chance. Give my kids a chance. Think about your little boy. You'd fight for him, wouldn't you?"

Seconds passed. A minute. Sara waited and watched him. *Slap...slap...slap.* Whatever was going on inside his mind had left his face blank. She didn't dare say anything else, didn't want to ruin her chances by pushing too far.

Another minute passed before he shoved himself away from the wall, crawled over to her. He took the key out of his pocket and reached for the lock.
Hesitated...hesitated...hesitated, then jammed it in and twisted.

The sound of the lock clattering to the floor was the most liberating thing Sara had ever heard. She scrambled out, nearly falling over when she tried to stand on her weak, throbbing legs.

He stood up beside her.

She flinched when he took her hand, but relaxed when he put the set of car keys in her palm, closing her fingers around them. "Take these," he said. "She's in my basement. The kids, too." He recited his address and then made Sara repeat it back to him.

"Got it," she said.

"When you go in, the basement is to the left, just past the living room, but you're going to need somebody with you. She'll know something's up if she only hears one person walking upstairs."

"You're not coming?"

"I have other plans."

She didn't know what he meant by that, and didn't dare to ask. She pointed at Teddy, who'd passed out during their conversation. "What about him?"

Michael looked over his shoulder at the crumpled and beaten body. "He was supposed to be the scapegoat."

"I mean, can I take him with me?"

"There's no use for him now. He can go, but you're carrying him." He untied Teddy, slung the soaking gag to the floor. Brought him close, draped his arm over Sara. He shoved his cell phone into her hand. "Her number is in there. Look under 'Sis'. You'll have service about a mile down the road, but *don't* call, don't you dare call, or you'll never see them again. Send a text. Say, 'Penalty enforced, ready for level three.' She'll think it's me and give you instructions. You really want to know how to beat her? Play your own game. She'll never expect it."

"How?"

"You'll figure it out. Now go, before I change my mind."

"I'll figure it out? Can't you just tell me what—"

"—I said go—"

"—the third level is supposed to be?"

Michael said, "I can't. She wouldn't—"

"I don't care if she likes it or not. Help me...please."

He exhaled, stepped back, and glanced down at his feet. "You'll get one more call from her on your phone. Then at the house, I'm supposed to bring you down to the basement and give you another note. Instructions like all the rest, and she's going to be tied up too, just to throw you off."

"That's it?"

"She mentioned puzzles, one for each of your kids, but she changes things at the last minute. I never know what she'll do until the end. In your case, the only thing that's certain is the outcome."

"What's the outcome?"

"You're dead and your kids are in a foster home. Same thing that happened to us."

"Dead? But she said—"

"You think what she *says* matters to her? You can't win. Not her game."

"Then what should I do?"

"I told you, play your own game, and that's all I can give you. Go. Go. *Go*," he shouted.

Sara nodded, aware that she was close to going back in the cage if she didn't get moving.

She used her hips and shoulders to pull Teddy along, shuffling through the cabin, struggling under his limp body. He could manage a step or two, follow it with a stumble. "You can do it," she whispered. "We're free."

They were halfway through the yard before Michael called out to her. "Sara," he said.

She heaved Teddy around.

He stood on the front porch, gun at his side.

Oh God...please don't...please don't shoot...

"Whatever you do," he said, "don't tell her I let you go. She wouldn't—she wouldn't like it."

"I promise." *Still trying to make her happy. Still her slave, aren't you?*

Sara bent and lifted Teddy higher, making her way through the yard, careful not to slip on the bed of pine needles.

The wind was calm. Trees stood tall and motionless overhead. Through the serenity of the peaceful forest, she heard the puff of air escaping a silencer, followed by the *thump* of a mass falling on wood.

She didn't look back.

DJ cursed at the rush hour traffic on I-5. He hadn't seen it this bad in ages. Radio reports indicated a three-car pileup. One overturned, serious injuries, paramedics en route.

I should've known better, he thought. It was always a gamble, even when he wasn't in a hurry. Fight the bumper-to-bumper exodus back to the suburbs on the interstate, or march from stoplight to stoplight like all the other zombies on the streets who were trying to get home.

Barker hadn't answered his multiple calls, so he sat in line, creeping ahead, inch by excruciating inch, using the delay to think, to analyze.

At the mention of the necklace, he'd rushed out of Willow Bluesong's house without thought as to where he was going or what he should do next. His first reaction was to be on the move, in a hurry to get somewhere, and now, sitting at a complete standstill, the lapse in judgment had cost him.

Lights and siren, lights and siren. Just get out of this mess. But go where?

Shelley Sergeant's place was the obvious choice, however unlikely it was that she would be home. But was she involved? Really? Her California DMV records had said her eyes were green. Not mismatched. Not brown and blue.

Wait...I didn't check her history...what if it was...

The Mazda in front of him managed to move forward, and DJ eased up on the brakes, coasted along with it. He called the station, got Davis on the line, asked him to check up on Shelley Sergeant with explicit instructions to look for anything out of the ordinary about her eyes.

He waited. He hoped. He crawled another two feet.

His cell rang, caller ID revealing it was Barker. He answered, "It's about time."

"Easy, JonJon, I got enough of that from my ex-wife. Looks like you were tapping that speed dial button with a jackhammer. You got something?"

"That necklace. The one the bartender mentioned."

"I thought you'd given up on that one."

"It's a stretch, but—"

"We live and die by coincidence, cowboy. What've you got?"

"Shelley Ann Sergeant. Sara Winthrop's assistant."

"She told you whose it was?"

"No," he said, rolling forward, "I think she was *wearing* it."

"What? How'd you find that out?"

"The Bluesong woman."

"The babysitter?"

"I figured I'd start the ground-pounding with her. Hit the high spots and then work my way out. Good thing I did. Anyway, you should've seen the look on her face when I mentioned the Sergeant girl."

"Could've chewed through leather, huh?"

"Fireballs out of her eyes. Here's the thing: she says that Sergeant wears this necklace with the letters 'S.D.' on it. Said she thinks it stands for 'She-Devil'."

"No kidding. She got that eye disease thing you were so hell-bent on?"

"Davis is checking up on it. She's from Cali, driver's license says her eyes are green, though."

"Liars lie. Whereabouts down south? You've got him looking for priors, don't you?"

"Yep. Last known address was...holy shit."

"What?"

"San Diego...S.D. Too much of a stretch?"

"I've seen less break a case wide open, so let's run with it. Bartender said the letters were—what was the word she used? Intertwined?"

"Right. Could it be a logo?"

"Possible. What has an S.D. on it down there? You know, for a symbol? Sports team?"

"The Chargers?"

"Lightning bolt, JonJon. You don't watch much football, do you?"

DJ ignored the jab. "The Padres? They have an S.D. on their caps, don't they?"

"That they do, but it doesn't give us much to go on. Check the colleges, too. Who's in the area? UCSD?"

"UCSD and San Diego State, that I know of."

"They use an S.D. for anything?"

"Texas, Barker. The only thing I know is orange and horns."

"Have Davis check into it when he gets back to you."

"On my list. Any news from your end?"

"Blood and hair samples off to the lab. Hunch says Rutherford, of course. But get this, cowboy, they dusted and found a full handprint on the window. Clean as fresh underwear. Big one, too."

"Amateur or not, he wouldn't be that stupid, would he?"

"The man walked away from a bloody car in broad daylight with a perfect handprint on the inside of the windshield. Either he's a damn idiot—"

"Or he *wanted* to get caught."

"Right as rain. I'm heading back to the station to check on the results. Where are you?"

"Sitting in traffic on I-5."

"What in the hell for, son? You're wasting time in the—"

DJ heard a beep over Barker's voice. "Hang on, Davis is on the other line." He clicked over. "Tell me you've got something?"

Davis said, "Did you figure this out, or did Barker?"

"The eye thing? Me—why?"

"Sounds like one of his left field theories. He must be rubbing off on you, JonJon."

Come on, any respect? Ever? "I'll be sure to let him know. What'd you find?"

"Car accident last year. Shelley Ann Sergeant of San Diego cited for reckless driving. Driver indicated that she wasn't wearing her contacts...officer noted a discrepancy between the stated eye color on the license and the actual eye color...doesn't say what kind...no citation for providing false information. Cute girl. He probably took it easy on her."

DJ felt a rush of blood surge through his head as he looked for an opening in the blockade of cars to his right. A rig to his left hauling a load of timber. Trapped. An ambulance screamed by on the shoulder, heading for the accident. He flicked on his lights, his siren, began angling himself to the right, forcing his way between an SUV and a furniture-delivery truck. "Good work, Davis. I need a couple more things. Find out where she went to school—"

"One step ahead of you. Graduated from San Diego State University. Smart cookie. GPA up somewhere around the moon."

"You near a computer?"

"I can be, one sec."

"Look up the symbol for their sports team."

"Their sports team? Which one?"

"Doesn't matter. Football. Look up pictures of the football helmet. Tell me what you see." A horn blared and DJ flicked a look over his shoulder, expecting to see a pissed off driver with the gall to honk at a policeman, but instead, an woman had stopped and was waving him over, giving him room to get by.

"Um...looks like...red, black letters...says 'Aztecs'...another one with 'S.D.' on it, sort of wrapped together."

"Bingo. Move, dammit!"

"What're you doing?"

"Sorry. Stuck in traffic. Damn idiots won't get out of my way. I need an address. Portland current."

"Let's see...121 Blaylock Avenue."

"Thanks, Davis," he said. He made it to the shoulder, clicked over to Barker, hit the gas. The engine roared, pushed him back in his seat. "You there?"

"Thumb-twiddling. Davis got anything?"

"Forget the samples and the prints. Sergeant's place, as

quick as you can." He recited the address, shot down the nearest exit ramp, and hung up before Barker had a chance to balk.

***

He made up time by ducking down side streets. Lights and siren off, but going too fast for the residential area. He almost clipped a cyclist as he barged past a stop sign, swerving around a woman backing out of her driveway. As long as he was careful, the dangers here were minimal compared to navigating the impossible traffic on Lombard Street, over where the pizza shops and bars and laundries kept a steady stream of customers zipping in and out of every gap they could wedge a car into.

DJ took a right onto Blaylock, and cruised to a stop two houses down from the Sergeant residence. Cut off the engine, surveyed the area while he waited on Barker. If his partner managed to fight his way through rush-hour traffic, sirens blazing, it would take him at least twenty to thirty minutes.

That's too long...too long. But I should wait.

What if she has Sara in there right now? The kids, too. Ten minutes, Barker.

Cars were parked up and down either side of the street. A plump jogger lugged her body down the sidewalk, her running clothes soaked through to the skin. Lights illuminated living rooms, dining rooms. He imagined families inside sitting down for dinner or parents leaning over algebra books, trying to help out a teenager, but getting just as confused as their children. It made him think of Jessica and the home-cooked meal he'd be missing. Again. She didn't mind. At least, she said she didn't. She never complained, never asked questions. Simply kissed him and made him promise to come home safe. Every single morning, the same routine.

And so far, he'd kept his promises. The closest he'd come to a body bag was a domestic dispute six weeks in as a patrolman. The pop of a 9mm and the subsequent explosion of a brick, inches above his head. Way too close, and he'd frozen in place, unable to *make* his body react.

That was the thing. You never knew when it was your turn. Poke your head through a door, find out what a bullet tastes like. He had a recurring nightmare about it being something simple, like a routine stop to ask a couple of questions.

In the dream, he walked into the same building every time: a beat down, rundown, decrepit tire shop. A red Mustang, late '60s model, sat with its hood up and a mechanic's legs sticking out from underneath. He'd think about how the legs looked like the Wicked Witch of the West's after the house had fallen on her. He'd walk up, poke his head under the hood, looking at all the parts, examining how they fit together, worked together, admiring how clean they were, how spotless. Then he'd twist his head around, noticing the grinning face of the mechanic looking up at him. He could see the 9mm pointed at his head and then would watch as the knife-shaped blast of fire escaped the barrel. He'd hear the *crack*, and then stare at the bullet careening toward him in slow motion.

Always waking up before it hit.

Always.

He understood the symbolism, understood what his brain was trying to work out. Or at least he thought he did. It mirrored his life. The questions, the curiosity, snooping around under the hood, trying to figure out how the criminal mind worked. The fear of getting caught by surprise, of not being able to react in time.

All justified and reasonable. Both his fears and Jessica's. He debated on whether to call her, let her know he'd be late. Decided against it, sent her a text instead, telling her it was going to be a long night, and to keep the bed warm for him.

She replied right away. Told him she loved him and missed him, and to be safe.

He smiled, checked the time. Twelve minutes had passed, and still no Barker.

He thought about Shelley, tried to scrutinize her profile. Atypical of what he knew and was accustomed to. Early twenties female, highly intelligent. Worked as close to Sara Winthrop as anybody could get. No real connection to the children yet, but it was close enough to matter. If she *was* involved with the kids, why go through all the trouble with the stripper? To frame Teddy Rutherford? Could be. From the way the people at the office talked about him, he was the obvious fall guy.

But what in the hell would a pretty little girl from San Diego have against her boss? Has to be something big to take it this far...pretty little girl...San Diego...

San Diego....San Diego...

Something blipped on the radar in his mind. Something else about San Diego. Something from earlier in the day. Something he'd read.

Where else did I see that? Barker...Barker...the station...Sara's husband...reading his report...San Diego...

Brian Winthrop had made a trip to San Diego just months before he had gone missing.

And the connection is...?

He tried to play out the scenario in his head.

Brian Winthrop takes a trip to San Diego...he meets Sergeant somehow...she's working the bar at the hotel...couple of drinks...roll in the hay with a younger woman...thinks he's in love...flies home, can't stop thinking about her...disappears like a coward...leaves a wife and three little kids behind...

Promising. Happened often—more frequently than innocent wives and families deserved.

But if that were the case, it didn't explain what Sergeant was doing in Portland, working side by side with Sara, kidnapping her children.

He knew what Barker would say: 'Only God and walls know why people do what they do.'

He checked his watch again. Twenty minutes.

Can't wait anymore.

He opened his car door, stepped out into the street. Slowly made his way down the sidewalk.

Dreading this part. Dreading the approach.

And then he was saved from doing it alone with the slam of a car door and a loud whisper of, "DJ, hold up."

Barker trotted down the street toward him.

DJ, relieved, said, "About damn time. What took you so long?"

"Had to stop and get you a fresh pair of panties," Barker said, patting him on the back. "She home?"

"Doesn't look like it. You think we've got enough for

probable cause?"

"Wouldn't bet my paycheck on it, but I'm going with 'ready, fire, aim' on this one. I think you've earned the right to kick the door open this time. Have at it, JonJon."

DJ nodded and headed up the steps. Tried not to think about looking under the hood of a Mustang.

CHAPTER 20
SARA

Sara dumped Teddy into the car, lifting his legs and helping him inside. He managed to shut the door on his own, then collapsed back onto the seat.

Before getting in, she opened up the most recent texts on Michael's phone, the ones to Sis, and read through. They had started that morning.

> Michael says: Packages secure. No trouble.
> Sis says: Good. Samson confirms.
> Michael says: Napoleon?
> Sis says: Convinced him. Meet Samson as discussed. Lose the car.
> Michael says: Enough time for Mother Goose?
> Sis says: Yes. Stick to the plan.

Sara could see that some time had passed between that and the next series.

> Michael says: Took care of car. Barely made it. She's coming.
> Sis says: Stop texting, idiot. CALL ME!

And then another break, followed by a series that must have occurred while she had been blindfolded in the back seat.

> Michael says: On way to cabin. Mother Goose out of

control.

Sis says: OMG, are you driving and texting?

Michael says: Yes drvng. Not sure abt this. Kids?

Sis says: They're ok. Do NOT text back. Drive.

Michael says: MG and Napo no prob, but kids? Too much. Can't do.

Sis says: You can and you WILL. If she gets out of line, use the penalty.

Michael says: ok you right. Jus dont hurt kids. Plaes.

Sis says: You will not order me, understand?

Michael says: Sry my fault.

Sis says: Mother would not approve of this disobedience.

Michael says: I no. Sry. But ples no pain for kids, okay?

Michael says: Sis?

Michael says: Sis?

Michael says: Sis?

The conversation ended there. Sara felt a cool chill ripple across her skin.

Michael had been struggling with abducting her children the whole time.

Sara got in the car, checked on Teddy, felt for a pulse. He was out cold, beaten and bruised, sitting in his own piss-stained pants. Dried blood was caked around his nose, and his eyes were as purple as plums, his lips swollen. The gag had chafed the skin around the edges of his mouth. Bruises the size of eggplants were on his ribs and chest.

His breathing was slow, unsteady. He needed water, and she wished she'd remembered to bring the rest of her bottle.

He'd gotten the worst of it. His pain, his torture, was

physical. Hers had been mental. He would eventually recover with the proper care. If he survived. She needed to get him to a hospital.

Sara cranked the ignition and sped down the gravel road. Trees and rocks and leaves and the stream flying by. She had no idea where she was, where she was going, or how far away she was from the city and her children. She remembered that they had originally been heading east. It *felt* east.

The sun, where's the sun? There. That way. West.

She checked the phone signal.

Searching...searching...searching...

And, just like Michael had said before he unlocked his own cage with a well-placed bullet, the familiar connection bars appeared about a mile from the cabin. She pulled over at the next wide spot along the shoulder and sat staring at the keypad. Once she sent the message, the game would resume, and she would be on her own again, trying to figure out how to turn the tables on a psychopath.

Where would I start? My own game?

She'll think I'm Michael...I can use that...misdirection...surprise her like they're doing in the Juggernaut storyline...the ally is the villain...

Or...throw her off...tell her I screwed up...the game is over...make her think I'm dead...

There's no game without me...if I'm dead, she'll have no use for the kids...bad idea.

Sara thumbed out: 'Penalty enforced. Ready for level three,' then took a deep breath, her finger hovering over the 'Send' button.

Get it over with. Quit stalling.

She pressed it, and waited.

Teddy inhaled deeply, opened his eyes into two slits. "Why'd you stop?" He tried to sit up. Winced. Grunted. And then fell back onto the seat.

"We'll go soon," Sara said. "Waiting on something. Hopefully it won't take long, then we'll get you some help."

"I'm fine."

"Teddy, you don't have to do that."

"My right arm is completely numb, and my heart feels like it's beating funny, but other than that—oh, God, when did I piss myself?" he said, noticing the drying stain on his crotch.

"Earlier, when you thought he was going to shoot you."

"What a dick. Who *was* that guy?"

"Doesn't matter."

"The hell it doesn't, we need to tell the cops."

"He's dead, Teddy."

"Dead? Good. He deserved it."

"He had...problems."

"You think?"

Sara could understand the sarcasm, after what he'd been through. "It's not an excuse, I know, but he wasn't really—he wasn't in control of himself, if that makes any sense."

"You're defending him?"

"Not...he was...I felt—I felt sorry for him."

"C'mon, Sara. Really?"

"How much do you remember? Any idea whatsoever how you got here? *Why* you're here?" She checked the phone. No response. *What's taking you so long?*

"You saw me, didn't you? I wasn't exactly coherent."

"But what do you *remember*? You were going to tell me who you thought the woman on the phone might be, right before he—"

"Beat me half to death? Honestly, I don't have a clue. Shelley and I left the office about ten o'clock this morning—"

"Shelley? You left *with* Shelley? For what?"

He angled away from her, sucked in air through his teeth, put a hand on his ribs.

"Teddy?"

"Something stupid. I should've known better. Anyway, I got in my car, and woke up in that cabin." He rubbed his eyes. "Can we go now? Those trees are getting blurry."

Sara checked the screen. Still nothing. She checked the clock, bit her lip, checked the clock again. "Couple more minutes, then we'll go."

"Fine. Two minutes."

"Shelley?" She didn't know why, but the mention of Shelley's name stuck out at her. Intuition, something odd, inexplicable. Strange for her to be leaving *with* Teddy, like he'd said. Shelley despised him as much as everyone else in the office. Had confided to her behind a locked door that he'd been hitting on her. Said he was disgusting. Distinctly remembered her calling him a pig.

Pig...pig...Teddy said the voice told him he deserved it for being a pig. No...Shelley? Not a chance.

She repeated it again. "Shelley?"

"For God's sake, Sara, leave it alone."

"Teddy," she said, her voice rising. "Whoever's doing this has my kids—do you remember me telling you that?

Do you? If you know something, if you have any idea about what's going on and something happens to them because you didn't tell me, I will *not* hesitate to bring your scrawny little ass back up here and finish what they started. Got me? Now, why were you leaving with Shelley?"

"Okay, okay, calm down. It's embarrassing, that's all."

"And?"

"She said—she came into my office after you left, said she was leaving early and wanted to know if I'd come have an early lunch with her."

"That's it? You left to go have lunch?"

"I thought she wanted—you know how I am—the way she said it...I hadn't been laid in about a week. Figured it was worth a shot."

Sara rolled her eyes. "And you didn't see anything out of the ordinary—"

Michael's cell chimed, saving Teddy from her scolding. Sara glanced down at the screen.

Sis says: Good. Sorry for the delay. Napping.
Sis says: She chose #1? You're not driving, are you?

Sara said, "Hang on, here she is."

"Who?"

"*Ssshhh*, let me think." *What would he do? What would he say?*

Michael says: Sry. Drivn slo.
Sis says: PULL OVER RIGHT NOW.

Sara held up a finger to Teddy, counted to twenty in silence.

Michael says: #1 yes Teddy taken care of.

Sis says: No names! How many times do I have to tell you?

Sis says: Wait

Sis says: How do you know his name?

Sara gasped. "Oh no, oh no, oh no." *Don't do anything to the kids...don't hurt them, don't hurt them.*

Teddy said, "What happened?"

"I think I screwed up. Oh, God." *Think, think, think.*

Michael says: Heard Mother Goose say it.

Sis says: Okay. Anyway, good job. You MIGHT get a reward if it goes well. =)

Sara didn't know how to respond. She'd recovered from the misstep, but what would a man under the spell of his psychopathic sister say to that?

Michael says: I've been good. Please?

Sis says: IF you're good.

Michael says: Back in a sec. Mother Goose losing it.

She said to Teddy, "That was close."

"What was?"

"Hush. I need to think."

Michael says: Ok, back. Crazy woman. Backhand worked.

Michael says: What kind of reward?

Sis says: Leave some for me. That's MY job.

Sis says: Reward? Let's see...

Sis says: Should I wear red lace or black lace? ;-)

The phone almost fell out of Sara's hands. What else had he kept hidden from her?

Michael says: Red!
Michael says: Please.
Sis says: MAYBE. Get Mother Goose here fast.
Sis says: Can't take much more crying.

"Time to go," she said. "Let's get you to the hospital." *And me back to the kids. I'm coming guys, I'm coming. Hang on a little longer. Mommy's coming.*

Sara started the car, pulled back onto the gravel road.

"What was that all about? The texting."

"Talking to her about what to do next."

"You're texting the kidnapper?"

"She thinks I'm her brother. The one at the cabin."

"Can I help?"

"You can't even stand up on your own. I'll drop you off at the first emergency room we can find."

"You don't have time for that."

"No, I don't, but—"

"Just get me into the city, drop me off at a gas station somewhere. I'll be fine."

"Teddy, no."

"Sara, yes. Conversation over—your kids are more important. That's it, *no mas*, end of story."

For as long as Sara could remember, it was the first sign of humanity, the first sign of caring for another human being other than himself, that she had ever seen from Teddy. It was unfortunate that it took something like the last six hours for it to emerge.

Sara choked back the lump in her throat. *I asked for him to die.*

She said, "I'm sorry."

"For what?"

"Everything."

"Those weren't *your* fists."

"It's more complicated than that."

"Honestly, I don't want to know. Just stop calling me Little One and we're good."

"Done." *But, I can't ever tell you how one-sided that deal actually is.*

***

Thirty minutes later, Sara pulled up in front of a well-lit Chinese restaurant on the eastern side of Portland. Lights aglow, parking lot filled with cars. She was nervous, anxious, ready to be moving, ready to get back to her children, ready to face the inevitable, but feeling torn, feeling guilty, feeling like she owed Teddy at least another few seconds. She told him to be careful, and to check in with her in a couple of days.

"Unless—" she said, "unless you see me on the news."

"Don't do that," he said. "Don't. Whoever she is, she has no idea who she's dealing with."

Sara shook her head. "I'm—I don't know."

"You want to know the difference between us?"

"The difference?"

"Self-awareness. I *know* people hate me, and it doesn't bother me. I get it. I can see why, and I don't care. I get a kick out of seeing how far I can push people, but you?

You're clueless when it comes to understanding just how much people respect you. There's a reason for it. And I can promise you this...if I see you on the news, it'll have some headline like," he said, using his hand to swipe across an invisible marquee, "*Badass Chick Thwarts Kidnapper.*"

"I wouldn't bet on it."

Teddy shrugged, opened the door, dragged himself out, one arm around his ribs. He took a step, said, "Sara?" and then leaned into the car. "Eight o'clock, Monday morning. Got some good ideas for Juggs 3 that I wanted to run past you."

He closed the door and limped away, shuffling toward the restaurant.

She envied his confidence in her.

The diners stared at him out the window. Confused, pointing. A man stood up and cupped his hands against the tinted glass, hoping to get a better look. Teddy waved at them and lurched toward the front entrance. Waved like he was the homecoming queen, perched atop the highest spot on a parade float. She couldn't see his face, but she imagined him smiling, loving every second of the abject attention.

She watched him go, looking after him with a little less disgust, but not exactly admiration, realizing that her arch-nemesis, the virus that had plagued her for so many years, might, on some planet, actually be likable.

Teddy made it to the doorway before he collapsed. A waiter emerged, cautious.

Go, before somebody calls the police.

Foot to gas, acceleration pushing her against the seat. She was gone, leaving Teddy behind, hurtling forward through a sea of taillights and neon signs. Knowing where she was going, but driving blindly into the coming storm.

CHAPTER 21
DJ

DJ approached the front door of 121 Blaylock, gun drawn and held ready at his side. The shades were closed and he kept a watchful eye for any subtle movements. When he was certain it was clear, he motioned for Barker to join him. Satisfied they were out of the line of fire, he risked a peek through the decorative, paned window above his head.

"Anything?" Barker whispered.

"Empty."

"Nobody home?"

"No, I mean *empty* empty. No furniture that I can see. Nothing."

"What? You sure this is the right address?"

"On file. Should we bother knocking?"

"Try the doorknob first."

DJ reached down, grabbed the cool, brass metal. Twisted to the left, heard the latch click, followed by the groaning of corroded hinges.

Barker said, "Saved us a grand entrance. Careful, now."

They crossed the threshold. DJ first, Barker following. Hunched over, intent, all senses redlined, waiting for an ambush. The shallow Berber carpet gave them the advantage of silence as they crept.

Backs to walls, shuffling from one spot to the next. Every door open, every room void of any signs of habitation. No toothbrush, no shower curtains. Spotless kitchen counters, spotless refrigerator, two empty ice trays in the freezer.

A single cup sat next to the sink. Blue and plastic. Bone dry.

They relaxed, holstered their weapons. DJ scratched the back of his neck, let out a huff of air.

Hands on his hips, Barker said, "As empty as my cold bed at night, cowboy. Now what? Any more bright ones?"

"I thought for sure..."

"Not your fault. Gotta go with what they give you."

"We should check for prints on the cup."

"Hospitals aren't this clean, but we might as well. I got a couple baggies in the car. Poke around some. I'll be back in a minute."

DJ stepped around the kitchen counter and into the living room. Pockmarks and dings and scrapes on the walls. Typical of a rental, like his own place when he and Jessica had moved in together. She said they gave a place character, showed signs of life. He had complained about the previous tenants' lack of respect.

He bent down, examined the carpet closer. No indentations from couch legs or tables.

Nobody's been here for months. Fake address. Where's she staying?

They could track down the owner, ask if a Shelley Ann Sergeant had ever been here, or had ever signed a rental agreement. But with a fake address given to the DMV, more than likely she would've been smart enough to use a fake name. Fake bank account.

She'd used her real name at LightPulse. They'd have a real address on file, wouldn't they?

She wouldn't be that stupid. That's probably not her real name, either.

So she leaves Sara's husband down south, moves up here, somehow gets a job working for her. Bides her time for a couple months...watches patterns...figures out schedules...snatches the kids...takes them back to San Diego...Winthrop has his kids back...everybody lives happily ever after.

It's missing something.

Damn it. The note.

He heard the front door open, moved his hand closer to his pistol. "Barker?"

"Hand off the go-boom, JonJon. Just me," Barker said as he popped around the corner, shaking the baggie open. "Got an APB out on our girl. Doubt it'll do any good."

"She hasn't gone anywhere yet."

"What makes you say that?"

"The note, Barker. The one from this morning."

"Meaning what?"

"For starters, I'd say you were right about the husband," DJ said, then went on to explain his theory about what happened to Brian Winthrop, and the possible reason that Shelley Sergeant was in Portland. He watched Barker nod, watched the flickers of comprehension light up his eyes, listened to him grunt his agreement.

When he'd finished, Barker said, "You keep this up, I might be able to retire earlier than I thought."

"Don't buy your plane ticket yet. We've got the who, and the what. The how is shaky, but the where and why...zip, zilch, zero. Can't figure out what this game has to do with anything."

Barker scooped the cup into the baggie, zipped it shut.

He said, "Sounds to me like she's out for revenge of some sorts. Maybe our buddy Brian talked too much about the wifey. Miss Shelley can't take it, comes up here to take care of business."

DJ crossed his arms. "Why not go after her directly? Why get the kids involved?"

"She could've knifed her in a parking lot somewhere, but what fun would that be? She's hell-bent on revenge, she'd want to make it last, hit her where it hurts the most."

"Sometimes your mind scares me."

Barker tapped the side of his head. "The more you think like them, the easier they are to catch."

"Then where do we go from here?"

"JonJon, I'm afraid I'm done chasing my tail for the night. Sleep on it, and we'll start fresh in the morning."

***

But DJ knew he *wouldn't* be able to sleep on it. Sure, he could go home, flop down on the couch, or eat another cold meal while Jessica read or watched another home improvement show. Then, as always, when something about a case was bothering him, the inevitable tossing and turning would lead to an hour on the couch, surfing the internet at 4AM, or checking the refrigerator to see if something new had manifested itself out of the cold ether. He'd crawl back into bed for another round of choppy, broken sleep, then eventually relent and head out to the garage for a quick 5K on the treadmill before the sun came up.

Instead of heading for home, as Barker had done, he

made laps up and down Lombard Street, thinking, analyzing, trying to figure out where Shelley could've taken the kids. He read the street signs, the same ones over and over. Stopped for a cup of coffee at 7-11, chatted with the clerk for a couple of minutes about how they thought the Timbers were doing. Got back in his unmarked sedan, resumed the slow march toward more unanswered questions.

What kind of game was she playing? A literal game? Figurative? Back at the school, Sara had taken a phone call, and had rushed out in a panic. Someone matching her description had been spotted naked in the Rose Gardens, and then there were reports of her running away.

This person was toying with Sara. Had to be. Playing with her, testing her, seeing how far she would go to save her children. Humiliating her because she could. Her game, her rules.

If Sara was running away, where was she going? On to the next demeaning episode that Shelley had devised? There were no reports or sightings of Sara since that morning. She could be anywhere. The kids could be anywhere. Tens of thousands of buildings and homes. Hidden away while Shelley got her revenge on a woman who had been nothing more than a victim of an unfaithful husband who couldn't keep his dick in his pants.

She could be dead by now. All four of them. They'd be found in the morning by some unlucky janitor making his early rounds, or a hiker who had taken a shortcut through the woods and managed to stumble across their bodies.

Don't think like that. There's still time.

How many cases went unsolved each year? How many times did a child go missing from a playground and never came home?

No matter what the number might be, he refused to add to that total.

Not them. Not this time. Barker will come up with something.

And what happens when Barker's gone? One of these days, you're not going to have the luxury of his intuition. One of these days, you'll have to think for yourself.

His ringing cell phone was a welcome interruption. "Johnson."

"JonJon, got a call for you."

"Davis? What're you still doing at the station?"

"Keeping you in a job. You want me to patch her through or take a message?"

"Who is it?"

"Said she's Sara Winthrop."

She's alive... "Put her through." He waited for the line to click over and said, "Sara? You okay? Find your kids?" *Please say yes, please say yes...*

"I know where they are, but I could use some help."

"With what? Where are you? What's going on?"

"I'll tell you when you get here. Right now, I need an extra set of footsteps. Come alone, because I think that's the only way it'll work."

Chapter 22
Sara

Sara sat on a park bench within sight of Michael's home. It was in a neighborhood that she'd never been to before, full of houses in various stages of disrepair. Missing shingles, sagging porches. Yards that hadn't been mowed in days, if not weeks. Trash littered the sidewalk. Shoes dangled from power lines.

If he'd been telling the truth, her children were inside, bound and gagged, crying, suffering, wondering why their mother hadn't come for them yet, wondering who this horrible stranger was who had been terrorizing them all day.

I'm coming, guys. Mommy's coming, but I have to be careful. Just a little longer.

She had wrestled with the decision to get Detective Johnson involved, but as Michael had said, Sis would be expecting two sets of footsteps if she really *were* hiding in the basement with Lacey, Callie, and Jacob.

Her heartbeat hammered in her chest. The ache to see their little faces again had grown to an overwhelming urge to *move, go, now*, but it clashed with the need to stay smart, stay focused, and play the game how Sis wanted it to be played. One wrong move, one subtle slip, and she may never see them again, whether alive, or—God forbid— dead.

Roughly forty-five minutes had passed since their last communication, and Sis would be expecting a call or a text, or something, to let her know that it was time to start the third level.

Misdirection, she thought. *That's my only play here. I don't have time to come up with my own game.*

She thought about all the times she'd hunkered around the large table in the LightPulse meeting room with a group of their sharpest minds brainstorming, plotting, hashing out ideas, trying to come up with a plethora of hazardous situations to throw at the laser gun-wielding heroes of *Juggernaut*. Given that luxury and more time, with a notepad full of ideas and a corps of experts guiding her, outsmarting the villainess would've been simpler. Not guaranteed, but manageable. At least she'd have a shot.

But now, alone on the park bench, mind racing, no matter what form of trickery or deception she came up with, it all led to the ultimate consequence that she feared most.

Something terrible that she would be powerless to stop.

The only path that made any sense was playing the final level with advanced knowledge of what she was going into. She had the information Michael had given her, but needed more.

She needed her very own cheat code.

Like back in the glory days of Nintendo games, when you could enter a set of keystrokes on the controller and gain extra lives. Game programmers did it before then, and they were still doing it. The LightPulse guys held contests to see who could come up with the most creative way to hide something within *Juggernaut*, and to this day, some of the winners had never been found.

That's my advantage. Her game becomes my *game.*

She opened the text window on Michael's phone.
Be smart, but play dumb.

Michael says: Stupid traffic. Sitting at a dead stop.
Accident.
Michael says: Mother Goose tried to convince me to turn
on you.

The reply came swiftly.

Sis says: Surprised it took her this long.
Sis says: How far away?
Michael says: Couple of miles. Be there soon. Kids okay?
Sis says: YES, Michael. Don't start that shit again.

Sara stared at the keypad. *How do I get her to tell me what's*
coming? What would he say?

Michael says: Just want to make sure they'll be safe.
Michael says: Tell me about this level again. Did you
change anything?
Michael says: Can't call. She's listening.
Sis says: You KNOW what the plan is.
Sis says: You disgust me.
Michael says: Sorry. Don't want to disappoint you.
Sis says: Too late for that.
Sis says: But sometimes I worry Mother hit you too hard.
Sis says: That hammer must have damaged your memory.
Michael says: It did. I remember some of it.
Michael says: Traffic moving soon. Please remind.
Sis says: Jesus, you're hopeless. Read this, get here fast.
DO NOT text and drive.

Michael says: Ok.

Sis says: Bring her down to the basement. I'll be tied up, too.

Sis says: You and Samson take the kids and leave. DO NOT forget to loosen my knot.

Sis says: Samson is no longer needed, got it? Kids, your choice.

Sis says: The rest is up to me. Can't wait to see the look on her face.

Sis says: Betrayed by her sweet little assistant. So much fun.

Sara stared the final text, hands shaking. The butterflies in her stomach thrashed around like they were on fire.

It had been Shelley all along. She had suspected, guessed, changed her mind, and then back again, but now she had confirmation.

Copying Brian's exact wave earlier that morning, that one slip-up on the phone, coaxing Teddy out of the office. And even earlier, back further, back to her interview, wooing Sara with all the facts she knew about her, all the research she'd done, her insistence that she only wanted to work with the best. The now-empty compliments of Sara's skill at her profession. It embarrassed Sara to realize how shallow she'd been. The flattery had worked. She'd hired Shelley a week later.

Next came the offers to run errands for her, pick up the kids, visit her house, babysit. Work herculean hours to impress her, to win her trust. Every single move made over the past couple of months designed to get as close as she possibly could to Sara, to be involved with her, learn about her, get *inside* her. To get revenge on the other woman because Brian wanted to leave.

The betrayer had become the betrayed.

The level of duplicity was incomprehensible.

Sara blamed herself for not seeing through it, for allowing Shelley into her life, for welcoming the evil into her home with open arms.

I couldn't have known. She was flawless.

The other phone rang beside her.

Be careful, be careful, be careful. You don't know anything.

She answered, "Hello?"

"There you are, Sara. I've been told that you misbehaved, that you had a difficult decision to make during the last level." The familiar, digitized, apathetic voice rolling lazily through the words.

"Can I talk to them?"

"When I'm ready. How'd it feel?"

"How did what feel?"

"Choosing whether someone lives or dies. You may get to make that choice again when you get here. Welcome to Level Three. I like to call it...*Consequences.*"

"You can call it a hot dog eating contest, for all I care. I'm sick of this bullshit." She was pushing the limits, she knew, but the vitriol was expected, and she hoped she hadn't pushed too far. Maintaining her façade might not be possible if she heard another yelp of pain.

"Now, now, Sara. These outbursts will not be tolerated. Don't forget who's in control of the situation."

If you only knew, Shelley. You've seriously screwed with the wrong woman.

"Can we please get this over with? Just tell me what to

do."

"Your companion will deliver you to the proper location. Then, and only then, will the rules of the final level be revealed. But, before I go, you do have a question left for this round. Pity you lost your chance during the last level. It may have been helpful, but you'll never know now, will you? For this round, the same rules apply. You may ask at the beginning or at the end. However, asking at the end may only be possible if you're still...*alive.*"

She pretended to stammer, to think it over. "I'll—I think I should ask—no, I'll save it."

I don't know what it'll be, but you better believe you won't see it coming.

"What a shame, Sara. Such a...such a waste. I was prepared to tell you the truth about whatever you might ask. But now that you've chosen, we must proceed."

She knew it wouldn't be allowed, but she asked anyway, to keep the ruse going. "Can I talk to them now?"

"I'm afraid not, Sara. Not part of the rules, but it does remind me that I haven't heard a scream in a while. I must admit, my ears do miss that beautiful sound. We'll see you soon enough. Maybe I'll let you listen along with me, and I hope you're ready for this," the voice said, then hung up.

Sara stood, walked to the nearest trashcan, and slung the phone in with the rest of the garbage.

I hope you're ready for me, Shelley.

***

While she waited for DJ, a young couple pushed a stroller past Sara on the sidewalk. Early thirties, probably their first child, one happy family on their way to years of laughter and smiles and more babies. Soccer games, gold stars, high school graduation, college diploma, and then bundles of grandchildren they could spoil rotten.

It reminded her of the early days with Brian. The plans they'd made, all the fun they'd had picking out matching outfits for Lacey and Callie, listening to the same princess cartoon relentlessly playing on repeat until the DVD gave out and stopped working. Brian had joked that the thing waved the white flag on its own and said something about how all DVDs go to heaven, except for that one, because it deserved its own special place in Hell for the hell it'd put them through.

And then their little baby boy had come along and the cycle started anew. More onesies, thrilled relatives, a fresh coat of blue paint on a study converted into a new bedroom. Brian couldn't have been happier. He brought home a baseball glove and model trains that wouldn't be put to use for years. Toy fire engines, plastic swords, and building blocks that had to be put away because the pieces were too small. Brian was still outnumbered, but he'd been thrilled to have another male on his side after living in a home dominated by estrogen.

Brian.

Goddamned Brian.

Two wasted years of pining for him, allowing her emotions to wither, refusing to go on blind dates arranged by her friends, checking the internet *every single morning* to see if any news had popped up overnight, consoling her babies with repeated refrains of 'Daddy's not coming home tonight, he might tomorrow,' after the bouts of depression and putting on a good face for everyone around her, after surviving on hope and good memories alone, it'd come to this.

This.

That one singular moment where she decided to say a silent goodbye to him. She looked up at the sky, grown darker now in the late evening. Sun setting, ready to bring light and life to another spot in the world.

Brian, if what he told me is true, and you didn't make it, if you're—if you're dead...I'm—I'm sorry. What you did was wrong, but you didn't deserve to die for it. That's—I can't imagine what she did to you and I don't want to, but you didn't deserve to die. I waited for you. Waited and waited and waited. It took me six months before I could go to bed without crying myself to sleep. Six months!

Did you really try to come back? What would you have said if you had come home? Would you have told the truth? Would you? Would the lies have eaten away at you while I went on, clueless and happy that the love of my life had gone through hell to get back to me?

I was a good wife, I know I was. We had a good family. We were happy, weren't we? Damn you. Damn you, damn you, damn you. Do you know how hard it's been? Did you think about what I was going through while you were lying in bed beside her? Did you? God. I hate sounding so pathetic. But I have a right to be selfish. After this, after what you did, I have the right. I do. You put us in this spot. You did it. Our babies are in that house with the psycho you left me for. You did it. You did it. You did it.

And you know what? It's time to move on. I think I'm ready. One of these days, maybe I'll forgive you. Maybe I'll put on a black dress and I'll get you a gravestone and I'll lay down flowers. I will.

But for now, you see that rolling down my cheek? That's the last one.
This is your fault...and you don't get any more of my tears, Brian.

CHAPTER 23
SARA & DJ

Sara watched the young detective approach from a half a block away. Shirt untucked, tie loosened, sport coat hanging limp over slumped shoulders. He looked like he'd aged ten years since that morning.

He recognized her, gave a quick wave, and picked up his pace. A mixture of concern and relief in his eyes.

When he got within a couple of steps, she said, "You're alone?"

"I am. Man, you look like—I mean, good to see you're alive. We thought you were—"

"Dead? It's not over yet."

"I've got a badge and a gun. They're usually good for something. So *whose* house are we going into?"

She gave him the shortened version. The Rose Gardens, the run through the city, the phone calls, Michael and the cabin. She told him about Teddy, but not about sentencing him to die, nor about the remorse.

DJ said, "Spent half the day looking for him. We thought *he* did it."

"I did, too. She was trying to frame him."

"Shelley Sergeant?"

Sara took a step closer, lowered her voice and said, "You figured it out?"

"I wasn't sure. Lots of guesswork, nothing concrete. What's your plan?"

"Let's go. I'll tell you on the way."

Sara and DJ trotted up the street. She explained what was going on inside, what she expected, what Shelley expected, and what the final level might hold. They stopped at a neighbor's hedge fence, ducking behind it.

DJ whispered, "I'm not letting you go down there by yourself. Not an option."

"With all due respect, Detective...*my* kids, *my* choice."

"At least let me—"

"Just be ready, okay? Hurry." Sara darted around the hedge and up to the front porch with DJ trailing, muttering about bad ideas and no respect.

They climbed the five steps, passing dead plants in cracked pots, avoiding the broken slat in front of the entrance. Sara felt like a criminal, an intruder, sneaking into Michael's former home.

She pushed the front door open, stepping into foreign territory. Held up a hand to DJ, whispering, "Step hard. He was huge."

DJ mouthed, "How?"

"Try to sound—I don't know—try to sound big. Stomp, but don't be obvious."

"This is ridiculous. Let me go in first."

Sara stabbed a finger toward the floor. "I said *no*. You go in with guns blazing and my kids are dead, you hear me? Stay upstairs and let me handle this."

"But I'm supposed—" DJ stopped, lifted his hands, let them fall. Hung his head. "Yes, ma'am, whatever you say."

"Good. Now pretend like you're pushing me. Make it sound real."

DJ stomped forward and shoved Sara.

She stumbled, hit the ground, and whispered, "Do it

again," and then got to her feet.

DJ stomped another couple of steps, helped her up, shoved again. Harder this time.

Sara tripped, reached out, and knocked a vase from a table. It crashed and shattered as she fell to her hands and knees. She yelled, "Okay, I'm going," and gave him a thumbs-up.

He urged her ahead. Stomped on the shards, heard them crunch under his heel.

Sara scuttled around the broken ceramic and over to the basement door, looked back at DJ, watched him press his lips together. Waiting, waiting.

He closed his eyes, tugged hard on his tie. "Go," he whispered. "Be careful. If anything happens, I'm coming down."

She reached for the doorknob, pulled herself up. Took one last look at DJ, mouthed, "No, wait here." Twisted the handle, and let the door swing open, screeching like a coffin lid as it went. Ominous. Foreboding.

She planted a foot on the creaky first step, paused, and stepped again.

Heartbeat quickening, ears going dull like her head was veiled in cotton, the temperature change of the chilly, musty basement prickling her skin. She plodded downward.

Down, down, down, until she reached the final level.

***

She smelled the familiar but foreign scent of laundry detergent first, followed by the sharp light of the single, bare light bulb overhead as she moved into the open space.

Lacey, Callie, and Jacob sat in the middle of the room, bound to chairs and gagged with white cloth. The twins bookended their little brother. Eyes puffy, red, and swollen from hours of crying, but otherwise unharmed from the looks of it. No visible cuts or bruises.

They all saw her at the same time, and pushed against their ropes. Neck muscles strained against skin as they wailed, "Mommy! Mommy!"

She rushed for them, arms open wide.

In the final second before she reached her children, their eyes shifted to something at her right. Instinct and a sixth sense registered at the same time.

Where's Shell—

A wrecking ball slammed into her ribs. Her neck whipped sideways, smashing her ear against her shoulder. Her feet came off the ground, she was airborne, and then her attacker speared her into the unforgiving concrete floor. They rolled together, bodies smashing against a cabinet, glass doors exploding.

Sara tried to move, felt a piercing stab in her side. Broken bone? Knife?

Dizzy, dazed, glass digging into her arms, she lifted her head and saw the behemoth scrambling to his feet.

Heard Shelley's voice say, "Upstairs, Samson. Go. Kill whoever it is."

Saw a hand extending toward him, the flash of light on metal, and watched his thick fingers closing around the butt of a handgun. He moved fast for his size. He flew around an old workbench and then thundered up the stairs.

Sara tried to sit up, but the dizziness and throbbing pain

pushed her back down. She listened to her children bawling as Shelley knelt over her.

Face to face, Shelley smiled. "Almost, Sara. You almost had me. Something felt *off* about the way he was texting. He always asks for *black* lace, and that comment about the hammer? Total lie. Mother never did a *thing* to him."

Sara heard shouting overhead. Two gunshots popped a second apart, followed by a single *thud*.

Next came the sounds of unsteady footsteps clunking down the stairs.

Please be DJ, please be DJ.

And then *boom, boom, boom* as DJ tumbled down and crashed against the wall. Left arm broken and twisted behind his back, blood pouring out of the bullet hole in his chest, staining his shirt. He spat out a mouthful of blood and saliva, then said, "Police," and collapsed into a lump.

His chest rose and fell, rose and fell.

Shelley smirked. "Everybody dies in the end, huh? Brian. Samson. You. Your little angels."

Sara mustered what strength she had left and swung at Shelley's head.

Shelley blocked it, grabbed Sara's arm, used her leverage to pull backward.

The glass dug into Sara's back, sliced through shirt and skin as Shelley dragged her across the floor, depositing her in front of the kids. They screamed through their gags and struggled against their ropes.

Shelley used her knees to pin down Sara's arms. Slapped her across the cheek. Yelled for the children to shut up, backhanding Sara across the other cheek. She grabbed Sara's shirt, twisted the material, and yanked her up, screaming into her face, "Where's Michael? Where's Michael? Where's Michael?" growing louder and louder with each repetition.

Shelley lifted her hand and balled up her fist.

Gasping, Sara said, "Dead. He's dead."

Shelley punched hard and fast.

Sara's nose shattered with a sharp *crack*. The room went white. Her eyes began to water.

"Did you kill him?" Shelley said, jaws clenched, teeth grinding. "Answer me. Did you kill him?"

Sara gagged on the waterfall of blood in her throat. Tried to swallow it, choking and coughing. She said, "No, he shot—he shot himself."

"Liar," Shelley screamed. She swung at Sara's head again, leaning into the motion, putting everything she had behind it.

Sara was ready this time. She squirmed out of the way and felt the blow grazing against her temple.

Shelley's fist pounded into the concrete.

Sara heard the bones crunching next to her ear.

Shelley howled, leaning backward, cradling her hand.

It was just far enough. Sara swung her legs up, wrapped them around Shelley's neck, and yanked.

The body followed the head. Shelley went tumbling backward.

Sara twisted and rolled with the momentum, tightening her leg-lock on Shelley's throat, squeezing her thighs together, choking her. Shelley flailed and kicked, hammering on Sara's legs with weakening fists.

Sara clenched tighter and tighter, waiting until no more

strength remained in the punches. She released her grip and clambered around, straddling Shelley, pounding a fist into her jaw, her teeth, her temples. Pounding, pounding, pounding.

She grabbed Shelley by the ears, leaned down, and pulled the slobber-drenched face closer to her own. Blood dripped from Sara's broken nose, splattering on Shelley's cheeks, running into dazed and groggy eyes.

Shelley grinned and slurred, "Do it. Kill me."

"No, I will *not* kill you in front of my kids." Sara ground her teeth together, digging her nails into the back of Shelley's ears. "I don't give a fuck about the messed up shit you had to deal with, but they don't need to see it. They don't need to see it. They're little, they're little, they're little," she said, thrashing Shelley's head around. "How *dare* you."

Shelley giggled and tried to break free. "But we're having so much fun."

Sara tightened her grip. "You told me I had one last question. Well, here it is, bitch. Are you ready to play *my* game? I like to call it...*Resolution*."

She slammed the back of Shelley's skull into the floor once, twice, three times, knocking her unconscious.

Sara fell over. Exhausted. Relieved.

Knowing she'd done it.

Knowing her children were going to be okay.

Knowing she'd won...the game.

EPILOGUE

Sara struggled with letting the kids out of her sight, even months later. Like most children, time passed differently for them, and the events of that day were a distant and lightly scarred memory. Something they referred to as 'Remember that time?' while Sara dreamed of dying in a cage beside Teddy's lifeless body, night after night. At the office, she was a frazzled mess in a well-pressed business suit. The only things on Lacey, Callie, and Jacob's minds were the inevitable end of summer break and the return to school in a week. She dreaded sending them back to where it had all started and had entertained the idea of homeschooling.

But life had to go on. She kept reminding herself that she'd succeeded, but peace of mind was not a prize that she had won.

The only thing that gave her comfort was a single news article regarding an incident at Coffee Creek, a female correctional facility nearby. It was vague, hinting at what happened to those who committed crimes against children. It was easy to assume that many of those women were mothers themselves and hadn't taken kindly to the new inmate. No names were given in the article, but Sara had a good idea of whom the victim might've been.

Miss Willow became a bigger part of their world, often staying over and holding Sara's hand at three o'clock in the morning, talking, and watching wisps of steam rise from chamomile tea. These impromptu therapy sessions helped

Sara sleep through the remainder of the night.

Sometimes.

Sara knew that someday she would emerge from the cocoon of regret and self-doubt as a stronger, take-no-shit person, but for now, the recovery process was doing its job, albeit slowly. But it was better than sitting in a padded room, bound in a straightjacket.

She'd started referring to Jacob as "Little Man," dropping his first name in an attempt to disassociate him from the memory of his father's betrayal. Some days, it worked. Some days, it seemed silly to try. So many of his facial features—his smile, the dimples in his cheeks—were all carbon copies of his dad's, making it difficult to forget and move on. One day.

Teddy, bless his narcissistic, egotistical heart, had returned to his normal self around LightPulse. Offending everyone in proximity, pushing the limits of acceptability, causing two of their strongest employees to quit. He'd stared Death in the face, and had come away from it with a renewed, invigorated sense of being untouchable. Jim had called Sara into his office one afternoon, asking for her counsel on how he should go about firing his own son. She'd talked him out of it, and, as far as she was concerned, she and Teddy were an inch closer to being even.

Besides, when they were on the private side of closed office doors, he treated her with the reverence and respect that had been missing from their professional relationship for so many years. He said 'yes, ma'am' and 'no, ma'am'. Liked to call her B.C., short for 'Badass Chick'. She'd stopped calling him 'Little One' as promised, and encouraged the rest of the senior staff to do the same. Yet another fraction closer to making up for playing God with his life.

And then, on a wet Saturday in September, she loaded the kids into the minivan, stopped to pick up Miss Willow, and drove to the cemetery.

Sara parked and stepped into the drizzly, gray morning, leaving them behind. The light rain sprinkled her face as she zipped her jacket higher to block the wind, holding the bouquet of lilies and baby's breath close to her chest. She trudged up the grassy hillside, breeze lifting the hem of her black dress, passing simple plaques with nothing more than a last name jammed into the muddy ground. Markers with elaborate designs carved into the granite. Ornate cherub statues placed by those with enough money, or enough care, to do so.

So much death buried around her. Such little time they all had. How many broken hearts were out there in the world while their loved ones rested peacefully underneath her feet?

She stopped at the gravestone she'd come to see, which was nestled amongst a group of plain gray rectangles with simple designs and simpler lettering. Sara swiped her rain soaked hair from her face, stared at the name carved into the rock. Knelt down close to it.

"You were a good man," she said, "and it wasn't supposed to happen like this. But how often do things turn out like they should, you know? I think about you a lot. I wonder about what you'd be doing, where you'd be right now. You're here because of me, and—and I haven't figured out how to deal with that yet, but I'll keep coming back until I do, I promise. Maybe after that, too. See you next week, okay?"

She laid the flowers down at the base of the granite block, read the words as she had so many times before.

DET. JONATHAN JOHNSON
"LOVED AND RESPECTED"
1977-2012

Sara stood, traced her fingers across the top of the gravestone, and walked down the hillside, back to her family.

Back to where they were close.

Close...and safe.

-the end-

ABOUT THE AUTHOR

Ernie Lindsey grew up in the Appalachian Mountains of southwest Virginia, herding cattle and chopping firewood, and has spent his life telling stories to anyone that will listen. He currently works as a freelance writer, and is the author of two additional novels and numerous short stories.

Ernie and his wife Sarah live in central Oregon and their first child is due in December 2012, a few days before the Mayan Apocalypse. They intend for their baby to save the world. If you're reading this book after 12/12, you're welcome!

***

I take great pride in my work and had a number of readers and a professional editor go over SARA'S GAME before it was published, but the occasional *oops* does occur. If you happen to catch anything and would like to point it out, please feel free to let me know at **ernie@ernielindsey.com**.

I'll reciprocate with a gargantuan thank you and sing your eternal praises. (Honestly, I couldn't carry a tune in a bucket, so the *singing* part may be a bit of a stretch.) Or, if you'd just like to send me a comment, you're more than welcome. You can also visit my website at **http://www.ErnieLindsey.com** to sign up for my newsletter, check out some poorly drawn cartoons that are certain to elicit an eye-roll or two, and learn more about me and my other works.

If you enjoyed SARA'S GAME and would like to support the author, nothing is more effective than word-of-mouth. Please give some thought to posting a review and sharing with your friends and other readers on your social networks. Thank you!

Ernie Lindsey
October, 2012

ALSO AVAILABLE BY ERNIE LINDSEY

Novels

GOING SHOGUN
THE TWO CROSSES

**Short Stories
(ebook only)**

NOOSE
MOCKINGBIRD DON'T SING
SOMEDAY

2663032R00113

Printed in Great Britain
by Amazon.co.uk, Ltd.,
Marston Gate.